Praise for stories in the *Space Empire Universe*

"Great read. Kept me interested from the beginning."

"...the story is good and the tension is maintained."

"...a very good story..."

"...Came through with a solid five stars. Marital and romantic relations were quite well sketched out... a realistic portrayal of characters in this world view."

City on a Hill
and
Sojourner

Two Stories from the Space Empire Universe
by
Michael J. Findley

Published by Findley Family Video

Table of Contents

City on a Hill

One

With the Earth slightly above the lunar horizon, Shuttle Three disengaged from the lunar satellite, LMC-II. Braking slightly with the main thrusters, the shuttle drifted from orbit down to the Lunar Mining Colony.

"Shuttle Three, this is Lunar Mining Colony Surface Com Center," the radio squawked. "You are 15 meters at 45 degrees, 3rd quadrant out of docking position. Do you copy, Jones?"

"I copy, Com Center," pilot Clay Jones, the shuttle's lone occupant, replied. Clay was a dark-haired, thin man in his mid-twenties. "Guidance system malfunction. Am backing off to retry."

"Easy does it, Jones," the radio squawked again.

The thrusters on the 2,000-kilo shuttle kicked up lunar debris next to the shuttle entry bay as it reversed its descent. The guidance thrusters kicked in, invisible in the vaporless vacuum, but gently pushing the shuttle back into proper docking position.

"Thought this thing was maintenanced to repair this problem," grumbled Jones.

"Seems like it needs to be rescheduled," Com Center responded.

"Where was I supposed to sign up for hazardous duty pay?" asked Jones. "I missed that line, I guess."

"The company says we're happy, healthy, and well-paid," said Com Center. "Position looks good."

The shuttle descended and the bay doors closed behind it.

"They make a pretty good return on their investment, it seems to me," said Jones. "Thrusters shut down. Lock on docking clamps.”

"Seems so to me, too, Jones. Docking clamps locked on. Relax, mister. You're home again," said Com Center.

"No thanks to the company," said Jones. "You can't tell me they don't make enough to supply adequate maintenance, sir. Those stinkin' lousy, --"

Radio communications were interrupted by a tone.

"You're on the air, Mister! Do you need any more D-20 infractions this month?" asked Com Center.

"Lunar Mining Company Earth Base Communications here," squawked a new voice, as clear as Com Center. "I think I just heard a D-20 infraction over the airwaves."

"Aw, come on," complained Jones. "This is only a 25-watt local transmitter. You guys listen in on every linkup?"

"You know that even local transmissions can sometimes get picked up by just about anyone on Earth, Jones," said Com Center.

"On a clear day you can hear the moon," sang Earth Base. "Is it really Jones again?"

"Mr. Jones offers his humble apologies," said Com Center. "Sorry he can't deliver them in person. He's got a priority maintenance report to file."

"Jones really should watch those intercom indiscretions," said Earth Base. "Don't the fines get a bit expensive?"

"You might try living like we do, Earth Base," said Com Center. It gets to you. The company could afford to make things a little easier for us up here, or at least fairly compensate us for what we really do."

"Try to see the whole picture, Surface Com," said Earth Base. "The company's deep in the loss column at this point."

"Maybe my link is bad," said Com Center. "I'm sure I didn't hear you right."

"Anyway," said Earth Base, "we're getting ready to transmit a happy, healthy miner message to all the good folks who depend on the Lunar Mining Company to keep Earth running."

"Say again, Earth Base?" said Com Center.

"A commercial," said Earth Base. "So make it sound good, boys. You're on the air in ... six seconds. Five, four, three, two, one ... Broadcasting live from Lunar Mining Colony, on the air."

*****

The full moon illuminated a large front yard as the sheriff quietly closed the door of his darkened squad car. Three men and two women already stood beside a parked van. With a nod from the sheriff, they walked up the lawn in silence and stationed themselves around the large living room window and front door.

John Winthrop had brown eyes. He was average in height and build, with thinning reddish-brown hair and a light moustache. Just turned forty, he sat in the one large chair while his wife Anne sat on the couch with three of their children, Brad, 8, Theo, 15, and Sarah, 5. Alice, 19, sat in a kitchen chair with the youngest, William, 3, in her lap.

John opened the Bible and began flipping pages when the phone rang.

"I'll get it," said Anne, still attractive in her late thirties, with shoulder-length blond hair and blue eyes. "You just find your place and start without me."

She hurried to the next room, kissing John on the forehead as she passed.

John stopped turning pages and began reading, *"Behold, I go . . ."*

"I'm sorry," interrupted Anne. "But Bob Michaels's crew has a broken belt on the shampooer."

John closed his Bible and started to rise. Anne stopped him with a gentle touch on his shoulder.

"Stay seated," said Anne. "Let me bring the phone over there. Just a minute, Bob."

John smiled at Anne as he took the phone.

"Which truck have you got?" asked John. "Weren't you supposed to take #22?" He paused. "You've got two small shampooers, so put Janet and Fred on them cleaning the kiosks and seminar rooms. The rest of you reverse your normal procedures and start with the trash. I have something here that will take about half an hour. Afterward I'll swing by the shop. I should be there in about an hour."

John pushed a button to hang up. Next he pushed another button for AutoDial.

"Iso isn't going to like this," said John to Anne while the phone rang. "I can hear him now ... 'Boss Winthrop toils from sun to sun, but a mechanic's work is never done.' Bob took the truck that's going into the shop tomorrow . . . Iso? Bob's at the Sheraton and he just started shampooing the main exhibit hall when the belt broke. He took truck #62. I thought I'd swing by the shop and switch trucks. I told him to take #22. What? Oh, I'm sorry. That was my mistake."

Anne took the phone.

"I'll have to let Bob use my truck," said John. "Thank you, Anne."

Anne returned to the couch and John resumed reading the Bible.

John started over.

> "'Behold, I go forward but He is not there,
> and backward, but I cannot perceive Him;
> When He acts on the left, I cannot behold Him;
> He turns on the right, I cannot see Him. But He
> knows the way I take; when He has tried me, I
> shall come forth as gold. My foot has held fast
> to His path; I have kept His way and not
> turned aside. I have not departed from the
> command of His lips; I have treasured the
> words of His mouth more than my necessary
> food.' That's Job 23:8-12."

Brad, blond and blue-eyed like his mother asked, "Is that talking about God, daddy?"

"Of course it is, Brad," answered red-haired, freckled Theo.

"If you know so much, Theo, what's it mean?" asked Sarah, tossing her light brown pigtails and staring at Theo with challenge in her brown eyes.

"Uhhh..." said Theo, turning his blue eyes away.

"It means we can't always tell by feelings that God is really there, right, Dad?" said Alice. John paused a moment, noticing again how much Alice resembled her mother, blond and slender, so quiet and earnest, yet with her father's brown eyes.

"Yes, Alice," said John. "God may seem far away in times of trouble. We may find ourselves searching for some sign that He's really there. But we have the promise in His Word that He'll never forsake us. He really is there, whether it feels like it or not."

"Well, these are times of trouble, all right," said Anne. "At least six families have asked for prayer because authorities are questioning them so much about our church, our home-schooling ... we need to pray for God's help and wisdom."

William, tow-headed, blue eyes dark with impatience, kicked the legs of the chair and struggled to get down. Alice gripped him tightly and he began to cry.

"Let's put Will to bed before we pray," said Theo. "We can't hear anything."

"Good idea," said Anne as she picked Will up.

"Don't wanna go to bed," screamed Will. "No! I don't wanna go to bed. No!"

"You must not say 'no' to your mother," said John.

John took Will away from his wife and spanked the child. The door flew open and the sheriff, two deputies, and three others came through the door.

"Who are you?" demanded John.

"What is this?" gasped Anne.

"Daddy!" cried Sarah. A social worker grabbed her.

"Leave me alone!"

"Let go of her!" Brad grabbed the social worker and tried to free his sister but a deputy picked him up. "Ouch! Daddy! Mommy!"

"Mommy!" screamed William in terror as a social worker wrenched him from his father's hands with the help of the sheriff. "I want my mommy!"

Brad and Sarah were forced outside, along with William.

"Quiet!" screamed the social worker. "Be quiet, all of you!"

"Dad, what's happening?" asked Theo. "What did we do? Are they taking us to jail?"

The sheriff handcuffed John Winthrop as he responded.

"I'm not sure, son. Try to look after your brothers and sisters."

"Mom," whispered Alice, "I'm scared."

"Pray, Alice," said Anne. "And take care of the others if you can." A deputy handcuffed Anne and pushed her out the door.

Porch lights erupted and doors opened in time for neighbors to see the Winthrop children herded into police vans. The Winthrops were pushed into separate cars. One deputy remained behind to padlock the house.

Two

The Lunar Com Center was no more than a large bump off the main corridor from the shuttle bays. Though roomy enough for several dozen people to stand, it had only four stools by the console. They were vacant as usual. Only a large, low-resolution monitor occupied the wall at right angles to the console. It showed a shuttlecraft approaching the Lunar Mining Colony shuttle bay doors against a background of an eternally unmoving Earth. None of the small groups scattered around the room paid attention to the monitor.

"We're not the first underpaid employees in history," grumbled one man, tall, dark-skinned and thin. "So what did other people do about it?"

"Look, they need us," insisted Joe Miller, one of the foremen. He was short, stockily-built, with tightly-curled brown hair and gray eyes that looked straight at a person, always calculating the effect of his words on the hearer. "Retail sales on that last shipment alone netted the company more than they pay all of us in space for a year, and that includes LMC-I. They can't interrupt their cash flow. They'll listen if they aren't getting their precious product."

"We've got the cheapest clean rooms in the galaxy," commented a short, pale-haired man with watery blue eyes.

"Along with the cleanest and cheapest silicon," someone put in.

"We've sure got enough of that up here," agreed Joe.

"I heard that Fujeaut closed its R&D clean room down a few weeks ago," said Mike Conners, a slightly overweight, short, middle-aged black man, looking up from a printout he was checking.

"Anybody left down there with their own R&D clean room?" demanded the first man who had spoken.

Two women had entered the room as the conversation heated up and stood listening. "Those things just bring in the pocket change," said Liz Diangelo, a redhead wearing a short, tight black skirt and gold jacket. "What about their precious RD_777? It's the base drug for every pharmaceutical company on the planet."

In the hallway on the far side of the room, the other woman approached a young miner with long brown hair secured in a ponytail tucked up into a baseball cap. He bagged materials and placed them in a container. She twined her arm through his.

"Come on, baby, isn't your shift over yet?" Her dangling copper earrings and loud purple bodysuit clashed with the omnipresent green jumpsuits.

"Yeah, well, these bags have to be packaged individually to withstand normal Earth gravity. It'll ship out next shift, and those guys will just load it without caring how it's packed."

"Don't expect some kinda productivity bonus for staying on the job past quitting time," said Joe, strolling by and glancing at the miner's work. "You know Corporate's just pocketing the profits, right Linda?" He pulled the girl's wild, bleached-blond hair playfully, and she slapped good-naturedly at his hand.

"Yeah, what's the point?" asked Linda. "You don't get anything for it. You guys work so hard, and take so many chances." She snuggled closer to the man.

"Figuring on raising your rates if we get a raise, huh, babe?" asked the miner as he put a bag into the container.

"Everybody profits when capitalism works like it should, right, sugar?" rejoined Linda.

"Come on, as soon as I seal this we'll see if we can't find something more interesting to do." He popped the lid into place on the container and allowed Linda to lead him away.

Joe met another man walking down the hallway from the opposite direction carrying a carton. Joe blocked his path in the middle of the room. The small, Asian-featured fellow was obviously glad for an excuse to set the carton down.

"How come they don't send bigger boxes for these things?" he complained. "This new generation of fruit doesn't fit in the old boxes."

"You would think they'd make new containers," agreed Joe.

"What?" laughed another man listening to them. "Spend money on the moon colony? Cut into their profits? Come on!"

"I'd rather have them raise our pay, anyway," The small man grabbed another carton and shoved it into place. "But I can't see them doing that, either."

"They just might change their minds if enough of us complained," said Joe. "We're just taking it. We gotta do something to get their attention."

"This is Shuttle Three," came a voice over the console radio, "requesting landing clearance." No one noticed.

"Com Center, this is Shuttle Three," said the radio again. "I repeat, request landing clearance."

"Hey, is there a shuttle out?"

"Huh?" grunted the pale-haired fellow who had commented about clean rooms. He wandered over to the console. "None of the pilots are logged out." He flicked a switch. "Well? Who is this?"

"Like I said before," said the voice. "I'm trying to land Shuttle Three. I didn't put a whole lot of fuel in it. Can we make it soon?"

"But who is this?" demanded the radio operator.

"Jon Newton. Excuse me. Newton, Jonathan A., employee number 63451. I was assigned to repair Shuttle Three. Repairs being completed, I took it for a test flight. Request permission to land this D-20 infraction shuttle.

By the way, who are you? Isn't there supposed to be a real radio operator on duty?"

"I am the operator for this shift," snapped the man. "Sam Aleti. Newton, you don't have pilot's rating. What are you doing flying a shuttle?" Newton and Aleti's argument had gotten louder. Most conversations in Com Center ended as eyes wandered to the monitor.

"Ahem, Mister Aleti," Newton began with exaggerated patience. "Pilot Viccieri is assigned to this shift but he's ... shall we say ... a little too well-oiled to fly. Pilot Jones is on temporary suspension from flight duty due to one too many D-20 infractions. Pilot Ting is spending his next paycheck on a ... ah ... lady. Not that I mind -- what someone does on his own time is his own business.

"All other pilots being assigned to sleep rotation, someone needed to test the shuttle, so I took it out. As to my pilot's rating, I was classed A-1 readiness for flight in the Air Force before I had an emergency appendectomy and got a medical discharge to spend six months recovering from complications. May I land now?"

"Sure, Newton," grumbled Aleti. "Come on in."

*****

The monitor showed the shuttle bay doors dissolving and Shuttle Three began docking procedures. The monitor image switched to show a middle-aged, balding businessman in a conservative but obviously expensive dark suit.

"Earth Base to Lunar Command Center. This is CEO Truman Solte."

Sam Aleti flipped one switch and said, "We read you, Mr. Solte. Please go ahead."

"Greetings from Earth, gentlemen," said the Chief Executive Officer of the Lunar Mining Company. "I'd like to extend my thanks for your hard work. The productivity figures for this month are very good. We're pleased with sales proceeds as well. Operations are close to full production, as I understand it." Several men entered the room when they heard Solte's voice.

"Sir," said Aleti, "as far as we're concerned, we are at full production. We're busting our ... that is, we're fulfilling all the quotas, and in many cases exceeding them. Frankly, sometimes there's not enough room to transport product in the freighters."

Jonathan Newton entered from the shuttle bay, the opposite direction from most other people. He turned his six-foot-four-inch, 220 pound frame180 degrees to see the monitor. His blue eyes narrowed at the sight of Truman Solte, and he stroked his well-kept grayish-brown beard. His close-cropped hair, a shade or two darker, was a little rumpled but he smoothed it mechanically and maneuvered closer to the monitor. All work and conversation had stopped, and by this time everyone was listening intently.

"Please don't misunderstand me, gentlemen," continued Solte. "Your efforts are appreciated. But perhaps you don't realize that this company was begun almost entirely with borrowed capital. It would be difficult to even list all the outlays the investors have made and the indebtedness this company currently labors under."

"No raises, guys," murmured Jon Newton.

"I've been made aware of the requests coming from the Colony for pay raises, and that's why I've decided to communicate with you directly. This isn't coming from my accountant, or my public relations director, or anybody else. It's coming from me. We cannot afford to raise your salaries."

Solte paused. "I'm sure that you have seen the retail sales figures for your latest shipment," he said. Many heads in the room nodded. "Unfortunately, even though we have seen tremendous growth in sales, we still are unable to pay our creditors, meet your maintenance needs and make your current payroll. The company is still operating at a loss at this time."

"We take a lot of risks up here, Mr. Solte," said Jon Newton. "Nobody really figured on just how many until we got here and started doing the work."

Solte glanced up, but could not seem to spot Jon Newton in the crowd. "We have upgraded medical facilities and safety procedures accordingly. All of you underwent training that as closely simulated real conditions on the Moon as our developers could devise. Each of you was selected for above average intelligence, education and skills. I don't believe many of you could legitimately argue that we misled or deceived you into signing the contracts you signed and agreeing to the wages set forth."

"Sir," said Jon Newton, "from our point of view, there's a -- well, a whole lot of money being handed over for our products, and a whole lot of folks down there depending on what we provide and wanting even more than they're getting."

"Who am I speaking to, sir?" said Solte. "Your face is familiar, but I can't recall..."

"My name's Jon Newton. I'm the maintenance supervisor here -- the guy who ties everything together with baling wire and chewing gum. We see the sales figures every month and they look real impressive to us. They're certainly higher than projected when we started this."

"Mr. Newton, gross sales certainly look impressive on paper, but it's not just a matter of dividing up the pie among you employees of the Lunar Mining Colony, or even the company as a whole. There are many, many creditors who want very big bites; but even they are second in line behind various governments collecting taxes. It just isn't all that big of a pie compared to the number of people we're supposed to share it with. But our board here has received a new proposal that we think might make the pie a bit bigger."

"I suppose you want us to step up productivity like good little happy, healthy miners, right?" said Jon

Newton.

"The idea is to change focus a little, Mr. Newton. We'd like to introduce a new product line and perhaps reduce work on some of our other areas. This is a new type of drug that's been proposed to us by a US government research facility. On the Moon it will be extremely easy to produce; by far the easiest project we've given you. And there's legislation being put into place that will virtually require the use of this drug. We should see profits pick up dramatically in a very short time. You gentlemen might even find yourselves doing less work and taking fewer risks than before."

"OK, Mr. Solte," said Jon Newton. "We'll string along with you a little while longer. But you'd better be right."

"Thank you for your patience, gentlemen," said Mr. Solte. "I realize that you probably won't believe me -- maybe you won't even understand this -- but we are in this together."

"Remember, boss," said Joe Miller. "We're not waiting forever."

Three

The congregation in the crowded basement divided into small groups. Men and women knelt in prayer. The children sat so still that few people even noticed them.

"Lord," prayed an old man who could not kneel, "we ask you to bless our elders, particularly John Winthrop and his family in this very frightening and difficult time. May he and his wife soon be released from jail and their children restored to them..."

"Oh, dear God," murmured a young woman with a baby, holding back tears, "give us strength to serve you and to do what's right, even when it's hard."

"Dear God," a boy said in a low, clear voice, "help the leaders of our country to do what You want them to do. Give them wisdom and strength to do right."

"We want to obey those in power over us, Lord," a young man said, shaking his head, "but we need Your strength in these persecutions..."

"Father," prayed a tall, gray-bearded man, "we know that all things will work together for good if we love You and follow Your Word. Help us to stand firm ... to be wise as serpents and harmless as doves..."

After more than 20 minutes of prayer, Carl Hodges, the songleader, a blond, athletic man in his early thirties, stood up. Several people stood with him.

"Turn to page 89, 'It Is Well with My Soul.'" Carl called out. "Page 89," he repeated.

As the congregation began singing *a Capella*, a loud knocking interrupted them. The man next to the door opened it.

"I'm Lieutenant Ward Anderson, police," the

plainclothes officer flashed his badge. "Is Mr. James Andrews here?"

"That's me," said a young, bearded man in a bright pullover sweater, stepping forward nervously. "What can I do for you, officer?"

"Sir," asked Anderson, "you are the owner of this house?"

"Yes, I am," said Mr. Andrews.

"I have here a notice," said Anderson, "that you are in violation of the city fire and occupancy codes because of the excessive number of people meeting here. This gathering is illegal under city ordinance #682, section 4, and #223, section 2. There is a fine of $1000 for each of these violations. Who are the leaders of this gathering, please? I'll need your names and addresses, and fines will also be issued to you."

"Wait a minute," said another man, wearing a tan business suit, "we've been told our church has building code violations, and we aren't allowed to meet there until they're corrected. Just where are we supposed to hold services?"

"Sir," said Mr. Anderson, "That isn't my responsibility. We just try to enforce the law. This meeting must end immediately, and all of you must leave, or I'll be forced to make arrests."

"There's no place we can go anymore, it seems like," commented James Andrews. "Well, no place around here."

"I see that you expected to make arrests," said Carl. "How many officers do you have? A dozen?"

"I was told that there might be some difficulty with you folks," said Mr. Anderson. "As long as you continue to cooperate, everything will be fine."

The men gathered on the lawn past the police.

"We'll just have to meet in smaller groups from now on," said Elder Leon Asahi, a portly Asian.

"Yes," said the pastor, whose name was Earl Collins. "Cottage prayer meetings. James, we're sorry about this."

"Well," said Carl, "I'm not sure we can take this much longer. Something's going to have to change."

"You men move along now," said Mr. Anderson. "Let's not make this difficult."

They obeyed.

*****

The monitor in Com Center showed the image of a 50,000-kilo shuttle landing to no one in particular. Only the three men on duty watch even occupied the dim Com Center. The shuttle docked, the bay doors materialized, the outer area pressurized, and the shuttle hydraulically descended to the main hanger area.

"What's this new equipment look like, guys?" the duty operator asked the shuttle crew.

"It's pretty much the same as the old stuff," Pilot Clay Jones replied. "We've got to get out of the way of the next shuttle."

The monitor cut back to an exterior view of the Lunar Mining Colony, with a second, smaller shuttle landing.

"That'll be supplies, right?" said the radio operator, turning to the two men at the counter. "I just got the inventory list. Have the next crew pick up the printout and start checking off."

The shuttle bay doors dematerialized and the 5,000-kilo shuttle locked on docking clamps and began descent as soon the bay doors rematerialized. The watch supervisor switched the monitor back to the large shuttle. A large piece of industrial equipment began moving out of the shuttle's open hatch.

"You really think these things are going to make a difference?" asked Mike Conners, one of the men unloading.

"I think that Solte's just trying to keep us working on something that will keep us from thinking about raises," said the radio operator.

Jonathan Newton walked into Com Center, sat on

the empty stool and asked, "Not impressed with the new product line, gentlemen? Notice they haven't tried making a 'live from the moon' LMC commercial for a while. It's tough to find a happy, healthy miner these days."

"We're not gonna be happy till we start getting paid what this job is worth," replied Joe Miller, one of the unloaders. "We gave them a chance. Maybe it's time to let them know we're serious."

*****

The worn, mismatched furniture was clean and orderly. It seemed to blend in with the small, well-organized kitchen and living room. Three elementary school children worked on lessons at the kitchen table while four preschool children played quietly in the living room.

"Well, Mrs. Lewis..." The small, thirtyish woman on the phone chewed her lip. She wore a long, loose denim jumper and her fine brown hair was pulled back in barrettes, falling down her back. She slipped out of her penny loafers and rubbed her feet one by one as she talked.

"... I'm not sure. I'm already home schooling, you know, and I have four other children to baby-sit. Yes, I know how much the daycare center costs. Maybe I could watch them for a week or so, while you look for someone else. All right, tomorrow at eight o'clock. Good-bye."

A soft knock seemed to awaken the woman. She hung up the phone and slipped on her shoes before opening the door.

"Clara Hodges?" asked a woman in a navy business suit, white blouse and deep red pumps.

"Yes?" answered Clara.

"This is a citation charging you with running an illegal daycare. You have no license on file, and no permit for a business. The amount of the fine is noted on the citation. If there are any children here besides your own tomorrow, they'll be taken by social services."

"Oh, Lord God…" said Clara. She placed her left hand on her mouth as she read the citation in her right. The caller turned with a rustle of her skirt and walked firmly off.

*****

The Lunar Mining Company's terrestrial boardroom appeared more suitable for a small family operation than the largest corporate giant on Earth. The only hint of power or wealth was the New York City skyline out the window. But even that was almost invisible behind CEO Solte.

"How is the new production line, the RD27851, going?" asked the CEO.

"After two weeks, they're just getting started, Mr. Solte," replied Hioto Mishito, a board member. "But I think we can still go by our original projected figures."

"Does that include the refinancing at the 10-year point?" asked Solte.

"I think we can do without the refinancing," answered the Comptroller. "We should be out of debt in only 15 years instead of 30 if all goes as planned."

"These are very conservative estimates," continued Gunther Klein, another Board member. "If the miners get behind this project, it could be even sooner. It depends on them, of course."

"They aren't very happy just now," replied Mr. Solte. "I believe that a raise in pay, even a very small one, would boost morale considerably. What can we do about that?"

"As individual contracts come up for renewal," said the Comptroller; "we should be able to give them what they want. But it would be a mistake to let them know that, in case something goes sour. It would look like we're going back on our word."

"I agree with you on that," said Mr. Solte. "When do the first contracts come up for renewal?"

"The first fifty miners who signed up are due for re-up at the end of the month," said the Comptroller. "That's a little less than three weeks away. I know this seems kind of sudden, but remember that only two months ago no one in this room had even heard of RD27851. For our bottom line, that really has been a miracle drug."

"Will you have all the numbers together to make them a better offer by then?" asked Mr. Solte.

"I thought you would ask that," said the comptroller. "The new contracts are already made up and I think the men will be pleasantly surprised."

"Very good," said CEO Solte.

"This still means, however," continued the Comptroller, "per our meeting last month, an across-the-board freeze on management salaries."

"Those men are more important," said Truman Solte.

*****

"This is a lot easier and safer," said Mike Conners, manipulating one of the new pieces of production equipment.

"Should increase production a lot," said a second miner. "Maybe double it."

"Yeah, but wonder how long it'll be before we start seeing more money?" said Joe Miller.

"Solte didn't tell us that, did he?" replied Mike. "How long's it supposed to be before the company starts making a profit?"

"Longer than I'm willing to wait."

"I'll go along with you on that," Joe snorted. 'This process will double our output. We won't see any of the profits, though. You just wait. They'll pay their bill collectors while we rot up here."

"They can't pay the bills if they haven't got product to sell."

Everyone stopped work to look for the source of a sudden, loud grinding noise.

"What was that?" asked Mike.

"The sound of an unhappy miner, gentlemen. I'm going to the break room."

*****

The rec room was the largest on the LMC, capable of squeezing in nearly 1000 people. It usually had less than 200 at one time. Today it had far more. The bar was normally sparsely occupied. Today it had twice the usual number of customers. One woman, a redhead in a tight black leather dress, moved through the crowd.

After being rebuffed by several men, she stepped up on a small platform at the front of the room, wobbling on gold platforms.

"Well," she began with an uneasy laugh. "Break time came early today, I see."

"Yeah, and it's gonna be longer than usual, too, Liz," someone yelled out.

"Look, I know you guys are mad about this pay business, but I think Mr. Solte's being honest with you,' Liz argued. "We girls have to make a living, too, and we wouldn't be here if we didn't think this was a pretty good deal." She smiled encouragingly as several other girls tried to sidle up to brooding miners. Several just turned away. Some actually struck at the girls.

"Sure, you got it easy," snarled Joe Miller.

"Come on! This kind of thing doesn't help," said Liz. "If you don't do your jobs, there'll be a lot of trouble. Be reasonable."

"We're running out of patience. It's time for some changes."

"Yeah, we're sick of waiting."

"We want better pay, and we don't want to wait forever to get it."

"Something's gotta give. The company's gotta get the message that we want action."

Voices got louder and angrier as comments continued. In a moment the rec room was too noisy to distinguish any individual voices. Liz stamped her foot and jumped down from the platform. Several women circulated, trying unsuccessfully to calm the men down.

28

Four

"John, it's good to have you back among us." Elder Asahi clasped John Winthrop's hand and shook it heartily. "Our prayers have been answered."

The dozen men in the otherwise vacant sanctuary nodded, looking relieved.

"Carl Sanders was able to get the charges against us dropped," said John Winthrop. "We're very thankful for that."

"Have your children been returned?" asked Elder Jenkins.

"Yes, that's a real miracle," said John. "It took some time to locate them all -- Social Services tried to give us a real run-around, but Carl's handled cases like this before."

"Too many lately," said Carl Sanders, a strawberry-blond man in a gray suit. "It's getting harder and harder to put families like yours back together, John. Your church still hasn't been approved to re-open, Pastor?"

"No," said Pastor Earl Collins, stretching his long legs. His expression behind his white beard was tired and grim. "The city keeps putting off the inspection. Anyway, we're trying to arrange some small group prayer meetings. We can't let up on the prayer times, even if we can't all meet together."

"I'll contact some of the folks who live near me," said James Andrews immediately. "They can meet at my house." Everyone looked at him in astonishment. It had taken all his savings to pay the last prayer meeting fine. "Pastor, there's not much else I can do for the Lord. Maggie and I talked it over. If times are better when he grows up, our baby's got to know what it meant to take a stand."

"We have to be careful not to bring too many people together in one place," said Elder Asahi. "They're watching us all the time."

"The children have nightmares of being snatched away again," said John Winthrop. "Social Services don't give up when they want to persecute."

"What can we do?"

"I'm planning to sell my home here and move," said John. "My father owned a cabin in Alaska which he left to me in his will. It's small for our family, but there's lots of land."

"Move!" said Elder Jenkins. "You mean just leave your home ... your business? How will you live?"

"We're going to try to farm and hunt. The land is rich in natural resources. I think we can make it, if we work hard."

"We thought of moving, too," said Carl Hodges, "after they frightened Clara by that threat to take away the children she baby-sits. But we don't have any place to go."

"Emmanuel Christian School was closed down, you know," said Elder Asahi, "and the pastor and principal thrown in jail. Social Services charged both men with child abuse for spanking. The pastor's children were taken away last week and he still doesn't know where they are."

"The school board called and said they were sending a representative tomorrow to review my wife's home-school records," Elder Jenkins said uneasily. "That's no kind of legal notice. They've told her all sorts of things they insist on seeing that were never mentioned when she filed our affidavit."

"Anyone who wants to come with us is welcome, but each family will be completely responsible to build your own home," said John. "Like I said, it'll be hard work. We'll leave by the end of the month."

"The Bible says the time will come when we will have

to flee to the mountains. But my ministry is to the sheep who cannot follow you at this time," said the pastor.

*****

The mixer the miner was working on snapped, throwing white powder throughout the room. He looked around, got up, and walked out of the work area into the rec room.

"Hi, Joe," said a tall, black-haired woman to the miner. She wore tight blue pants and a pink halter-top. "What're you doing here? This isn't your break time."

"I had a little accident, Kristy," said Joe Miller. "I cut my hand and I need to check it in the light. Here, you wanna look? Maybe you can make it all better for me." As he sat down, other men in the room looked around and chuckled.

"You didn't break anything, now, did you, Joe?" asked the heavyset, black-bearded man Joe sat next to.

"What's it to you if I did?" snapped Joe.

"Oh, I broke something, too." The man grinned. "Actually, quite a few somethings."

"Me, too," said a short, gray-haired man.

Kristy looked worried as all of the men in the room laughed.

"Yeah, I broke the machine I was working on," said a thin, pale young man. "Funny, how accidents sometimes happen." As they broke into another round of laughter, a buzzer sounded.

"Shift's over."

A number of men walked through the rec room on their way to the workroom. Some stopped to talk to the miners already there.

"There's no hurry about getting to work, is there?"

"Nah. There aren't enough machines to go around, anyway. One of them broke, somehow."

Everyone laughed. Many of the incoming men sat down and did not go to work.

"Mommy, where's the bathroom?" asked a blond-haired girl. She tugged at her mother, who was already trying to manage two smaller children and a baby. "I have to go now."

"Craig," breathed the mother to her husband, who looked helplessly around. "When you said we were going to the mountains, I didn't think you meant a wilderness without even any buildings!"

"There's no cleared land to even plant gardens," whispered an older man.

"Attention, please, everyone," called John Winthrop. He stood up on the huge stump that marked the end of the dirt road in front of his small cabin. "Welcome to the *New Hope* Settlement. Now, some of you look tired and discouraged already. Let me assure you, it's going to take a lot of work to make a settlement here. I can only give you the land and share my tools. We'll have to put in a lot of effort to make this work. Let's pray and ask the Lord to help us."

"We'll need the help, that's for sure," said Craig.

Perhaps a dozen men knelt to pray while twice that many remained standing. John Winthrop remained standing, looked to heaven and led them in prayer. When they had finished, Anne Winthrop squeezed her husband's hand and pulled her two girls aside, whispering to them.

"Come on, Abbie," Sarah Winthrop said to the blond girl. "You can use my grampa's bathroom. It's in that neat little house with the moon in the door."

Anne took Abbie's baby brother from her fearful mother. "Alice and I will watch your children while you and Craig set up your tents, Diane," she offered. Alice quickly took the two toddlers by the hand. Diane relaxed a little, smiled, and followed her husband off to sort through the mountains of baggage.

*****

"I've invited you here to keep you posted on the

RD_777 and RD27851 crisis," said the moderator at the meeting of senior pharmacists in Dallas, Texas. "With such an inexpensive, safe, almost foolproof base and antireactant so readily available, we seem to have forgotten a lot of old-fashioned basic chemistry."

The audience, made up of several thousand pharmacists, sat in rapt attention. The speaker adjusted his glasses and glanced at his notes.

"At this point, we have not had any reported deaths, but we must not take anything for granted. On-line databases listing drug interactions are almost impossible to access. I pray that none of you have been so foolish as to discard your older reference material on mixing drugs and their interactions." An uneasy murmur ran through the crowd. The speaker glanced up but hastily went back to his notes.

"We have been able to track down a number of commercial copies of software on drug interactions. These are available on tables in the back as you leave. They have been out of circulation for several years because they were treated as obsolete, but we can get as many copies as are needed. Um -- Let's open the floor to questions."

Hundreds of hands shot up. The moderator cringed, but stayed where he was.

"I can see this will take some time. Please try to limit yourselves to one question apiece and please, no repeats. Now we'll start right here. Yes...?"

*****

"Mr. Solte," said the head of marketing to the full board. "The last freighter was only half-full. If we are unable to correct these shortages, we will be out of business."

"We have thousands of complaints about deliveries not made, some pre-paid. Critical shortages are occurring in hospitals, research facilities --."

"We're only making enough money to meet payroll.

We won't be able to make any payments on debts this month."

"I'll talk to the colony again," said Solte.

*****

"Yeah, we're here, Mr. Solte," said Drew Corby, the longhaired radio operator in the crowded lunar com op room. "What's the problem?"

"Gentlemen," said Mr. Solte, "this is not the way to get what you want. You are cutting your own throats by these production slowdowns."

"Oh, you noticed?" said Corby.

"Mr. Solte," said Jon Newton. "I think this has gone far enough. We're ready to deal."

"There might not be any company left to deal with," said Mr. Solte. "This business was hanging by a thread as it was. You may have destroyed any hope of success. We've got to have full production restored immediately. Not only can I not increase your pay, but these production slowdowns might end all of our jobs."

"Look," countered Jon. "We just want to make some kind of reasonable agreement. Give us a time frame if we restore production to normal." Several other men murmured agreement. Others began to argue. Jon stepped closer to the monitor speakers.

"I'm afraid that's impossible," said Mr. Solte. "You don't understand what you've done. Several people have died because products aren't being delivered. We're facing massive lawsuits and breach of contract actions. We are unable to make our payments this month, but you will still receive your paychecks."

"Surely you can give us some hope of changes," persisted Jon. The rising voices behind him made him strain to hear Solte.

"Yes I can," said Mr. Solte. "We might be forced into closing down the LMC. There's nothing I can do except beg you to restore production and be patient. I'll try to work up some kind of time estimate when we can talk again about raises, but-"

Jon Newton turned away in frustration. The noise level in the com op room rose to where Solte could no longer be heard. One miner pounded his fist on a wall and walked out.

*****

"I have a letter here to read to you," said Pastor Earl Collins to his congregation one Sunday morning two weeks after the *New Hope* group had left. "Perhaps it won't come as a surprise, after all that's been happening. Our tax exempt status has been revoked."

"What does that mean, Pastor?" called out one man about half way back.

"Tax exemption," said Pastor Collins, "means that in the past religious organizations haven't been required to pay taxes on their property and income. The government has decided they could use all that tax money, so now they're going to tax us."

"How can they do that?" asked Elder Asahi.

"The letter says," answered the Pastor, "That by allowing us to be tax exempt they're supporting us, therefore violating the First Amendment. Anyway, this means that from now on we're required to pay taxes. Not just current taxes, but also back taxes. From a practical standpoint, it means that the Federal government is going to steal the property of all the churches in this country."

Five

The LMC boardroom looked neat, Spartan, exactly as it had last week, last month, and last year. The board members and officers, however, looked more tired and tense each time they met.

"Mr. Solte," said the VP of Finance, "you've seen the latest communications. We're almost 90 days past due on two notes and at least one creditor has begun legal action to attach our assets. We're on the verge of a Chapter 11."

"Those men," said Gunther Klein, "had their chance to cooperate. Instead they've sabotaged more equipment, creating more severe shortages."

"There doesn't seem to be any choice but to replace them," said Hioto Mishito.

"Yes," said Mr. Solte, looking at a slip of paper just handed to him. "As I expected, the vote was unanimous. May I introduce Mr. Conrad of the president's staff, and General Owens. They will brief us on the plan to forcibly evacuate the miners from the colony."

A door opened and General Owens, with Mr. Conrad following, entered and began shaking hands with board members.

"Members of the board," said Mr. Solte, "you must choose replacements. These men will take the responsibility of removing the existing miners."

"I'm sorry that it has come to this," said the VP of Finance, "but we can't say that it was unexpected. There was always an element of unrest up there."

"I think it was a mistake to take a lot of single men and prostitutes and try to make a stable organization," said Board Member Enrico Sanchez.

"Since mining began, it's traditionally been a job for

a family man who's got someone else to think about besides himself," said Klein.

"We'll follow-up on these ideas later," said Solte. He turned to Mr. Conrad and General Owens. "Meanwhile, you gentlemen may begin. Here is our space facility."

The lights dimmed slightly. A small wire-frame layout of the Lunar Mining Colony appeared over the board room table, including the LMC I, LMC II, their orbits, the Earth and the Moon. General Owens moved closer, gray eyebrows knitting, experienced eyes already assessing tactical options.

*****

"Don't you think we're going too far?" asked Jon Newton. "Maybe Mr. Solte was right."

"Shut up, Newton. We're not backing down now."

Half a dozen miners stood in the hallway by the com op room.

"They'll give in. You'll see. I've arranged for a little stronger demonstration of our seriousness about this," Joe Miller said.

"Make your demonstration as serious as you want," shrugged Jon. "Just make sure no one gets hurt."

"Nobody's going to get hurt," snorted Mike Conners. "It'll just make the point we all want to make. We're going to get what we want, or they're going to lose a lot more of their investment."

"I'm headed up to LMC-II to fix the inner coupling on docking clamp D. The replacement hose just came in," Jon told them. "Don't get crazy while I'm gone, okay?"

"It's a good thing you're leaving, Jon, if you aren't really with us," snapped Joe.

"It's not that I don't agree with you," protested Jon. "But you've got to be careful. Things could get 'way out of hand. Fighting over a pay raise isn't worth killing someone. If anyone gets hurt, this whole thing could backfire."

"Relax. Everything's gonna be fine."

*****

"What are you doing?" Carl Sanders halted his early morning jog in front of the church lawn. He wore a faded purple and orange sweat suit that had at one time said 'Suns.' Though he was obviously winded from his workout, his close-cropped blond hair still seemed to be in place.

"My job," said the portly, gray-suited man. He continued pounding a stake with a notice board into the front lawn of the church.

"I think you've made a mistake," said Carl, staring at the "Tax Sale" sign. "This is our land."

"No mistake," said the gray-suited man, wheezing a little as he bent over and wiggled the sign to make sure that it was secure in the ground. "I've put out nearly 200 of these signs and I've got almost 100 to go. Some Washington bureaucrats came up with this bright idea to pay all the local tax collectors to go out and put up these signs." He straightened up and smiled confidently. "This won't be yours for long."

"We paid off the mortgage last year," insisted Carl. He wiped his head with a towel draped over his neck. "It should be ours for quite some time -- forever."

"Until the auction," said the tax collector, waddling back to a small pickup truck with a pile of signs in the back. "You owe quite a chunk in back taxes, with a little over 2 months to come up with it. They don't think that very many of these churches will be able to come up with that much change all at once. Have a nice day."

*****

"George, what's happened?" asked John Winthrop. "Where are the supplies?"

George Raymond, a balding, thin, dark-skinned man, shut off the misfiring, noisy engine and leaned back, not even bothering to open the door of the rusting pickup truck.

"John," said George, "I tried to write a check, and the hardware store said it was no good. I went to the bank and they said the IRS has seized our church account as part payment of delinquent taxes on the church back home. I checked on my own account, and my money's gone too. The bank manager is sure it will be the same for everyone here. It seems that the IRS has invented some new taxes, moved in and cleaned us all out without even telling us."

"It can't be!" cried an elderly man. "All my savings -- I'm going into town."

"Adolphus, wait," said Elder Jenkins, the passenger in the pickup. "Some people in town think that we've started a dangerous cult out here --"

"-- Caching weapons and who knows what else," shuddered George. "They don't want us coming in to the town."

"How can we keep living out here -- how will we finish our homes --?" asked Maggie Andrews.

*****

General Owens and Mr. Conrad stood flanking Mr. Solte. Board member Hioto Mishito stood beside them with a pointer, using the wireframe projection to explain the details of the LMC.

"The Setup of LMC is fairly simple, gentlemen," said Truman Solte. "Our headquarters is here in New York and, as you know, there are branches all over the world where supplies and equipment are shipped out and product and ore from the moon are received."

*****

"Shuttles carry loads daily up to space station LMC-I, in low Earth orbit." Hioto picked up immediately after Mr. Solte stopped speaking. "At LMC-1 products from the Moon are properly routed and supplies to the moon are transferred to the large transports, which make runs to and from the lunar space station, LMC-II."

"Lunar shuttles meet them at the Moon station, supplies are unloaded, the colony's production is loaded, and the transports return to the Earth station, where cargo for Earth is brought down in the shuttles."

"Are the employees on these satellites targeted as part of the operation?" asked the general.

"There's no evidence that any of those employees have participated in the sabotage or slowdowns," said Mr. Solte. "We rotate men from the colony to LMC-II, and men from Earth to LMC-I, but the shifts haven't changed since before these problems began, so I see no need to take action against any of the satellite crews."

"Let's take a look at the detailed layouts of the moonside facility itself," said Mr. Conrad. "Mr. Solte, we'll concentrate our planning there."

"Certainly," said Mr. Solte. "The Moonside Facility consists of this central above-ground hangar, where the shuttles enter and exit." As he spoke the wireframe model morphed into a wireframe of just the Lunar Mining Colony.

"There are only two other entrances without cutting through rock," said Mr. Mishito. "One is over here by the Agricultural Center, and the other is by the antenna array.

"Both of these entrances would allow no more than a three-man shuttle. If you did cut through rock into the facility, the Colony is divided into more than 200 separate airtight compartments. Most of the miners would be here in the work/rec area. These are the living quarters, this is agricultural, this is the nuclear reactor core and this is the active mining area. The automated mining equipment is dangerous. Stay away from it. Besides, there shouldn't be anyone in that area if the timing is right."

Both Mr. Conrad and the General leaned over the table for closer inspection.

*****

A short, stocky figure stepped quickly out of the lighted doorway into the darkened room. The glow from the control panels of the Moon Colony's steam generator allowed him to see without turning on the main lights. He had no wish to attract attention. He pulled out a diagram, and made several checks. He walked over to the secondary steam pipes and turned a valve. As one warning light turned yellow, the man left hurriedly.

*****

The bare LMC board room looked even more stark, empty of holographic images and visitors. Lights began to come on in the darkening NYC skyline, but no one in the room noticed as they stared at the monitor, exhausted.

"Mr. Solte," said the VP of Public Relations, "these are excerpts from messages that we have received over the past few weeks."

An M.D. seated at a desk in front of a large medical library said, "Nearly ten years ago you introduced RD-121. It was very expensive, but it worked. Finally we had a base to safely mix almost 75% of all pharmaceuticals. With RD-121, dangerous drug interactions almost became a thing of the past. With your recent introduction of RD27851, 95% of all medications could be safely combined. The savings, particularly in underdeveloped countries, have been incalculable. Without RD27851, or RD-777, we are, on a worldwide scale, unable to guarantee the safety of most prescriptions."

A man in a three-piece pinstripe suit with bank tellers in the background and bare, windswept trees visible out the large windows flanking him tried to speak calmly. "Our computer has been down for six weeks. Over 1,000 employees have been laid off. Every ATM in Virginia is down. Alternate vendor parts are on a three month backlog."

A woman stood on a hospital balcony overlooking San Francisco Bay. "We are supplementing hospital staffs with university computer systems, professors and graduate assistants just to insure the safety of the most critical patients," she said sternly. "May we remind the LMC of the liabilities you are accruing?"

"Food processing plants are laying off workers because of these delays," said a bulging, middle-aged man with a yellow hard hat and an ill-fitting sports coat. He walked down a narrow aisle past a machine spitting out boxes. The logo of a major Louisiana packing plant was visible behind him.

"We can't process food without preservatives. As good as RD-777 is, we are contemplating a reversion to older preservatives. Since the conversion process will be difficult and expensive, we will be looking to your company to facilitate the transition to a permanent arrangement. We also expect remuneration from LMC for creating this situation."

A Social Service director representing a Chicago soup kitchen said, "We've got critical shortages because food isn't getting processed. You put your competition out of business. Now, when do we get our orders filled?"

*****

New Hope Settlement grew very slowly despite superhuman effort and cooperation from every settler. Day by day everyone continued to work, exhausting the few supplies they had brought and sensing the cold of snow in the air.

By now every family had a rough shelter and a source of heat, but no more. A small group of settlers presided over a smokehouse, busily curing a few animals, birds and fish and hanging them in the open.

The men rationed their bullets. Time and time again they attempted to repair tools. The women shared the task of washing well-worn clothes at the wringer washers under a bark lean-to.

The believers who had not left for *New Hope* argued with their children. School officials and law enforcement officers confronted them almost daily. Possessions disappeared, taken for back taxes on the church. Both groups of believers prayed earnestly.

43

Six

Three LMC board members sat with their wives watching
the late network news. The onscreen reporter squinted
slightly. She was short, blond, and wore a peach dress
and too much makeup.

"We're reporting live from this small town on the
edge of the Alaskan wilderness," said the broadcaster.
"Somewhere in among those trees a group of people has
started a settlement they call *New Hope*. These people
belong to a strict religious sect. They claim God has
commanded them to separate themselves from what they
term 'worldly influences.' They came here in peace, they
say, and maintain that the government is persecuting
them. It is difficult to obtain any hard information about
them, but it is known that their properties, including
bank accounts, have been seized for tax evasion."

The camera showed the settlement in the distance.
Everyone visible hurried about their work. The
broadcaster continued with a voiceover.

"Government officials have expressed concern, citing
examples of cult activists separating themselves from the
general populace and becoming suicidal or violent.
Investigations are under way to determine if active
intervention is needed to insure that no mass suicides or
'holy wars' result."

The camera cut to a shot of the reporter, wearing a
trenchcoat, her hair and clothing whipping in a sharp
wind as she approached a man in camouflage coming out
the door of a sporting goods store.

"We've heard that the people here in Abbyville are
upset by the presence of the *New Hope* settlement. How

do you feel about this group settling so close to your town?"

"They hunt like a lot of us," the man shrugged, removing his orange cap. "I ain't seen no piles of guns, but folks say they might have 'em."

The camera transitioned to the reporter approaching a young woman pushing a grocery cart across a parking lot. Frost was visible on many of the cars in the background. "Ma'am, don't the activities of the people of *New Hope* strike you as strange?"

"They seem kinda hard on their kids…, " the woman said uncertainly. "I mean, there can't be much time for fun with all the chores they do."

The next cut showed the reporter bundled up with a heavy fur coat and Russian-style hat. Flurries of snow appeared here and there. She appeared to chase a small old man to his car. Once safely inside, he rolled down his window to talk, his breath white puffs in the cold air.

"Sir, aren't people fearful of the *New Hope* settlers trying to force you to join them in their radical beliefs and practices?"

"They sure talk a lot about God," he shuddered. "Like He was really there, or somethin'. Makes you feel creepy. I don't want no part of them."

The camera cut to a shot of the reporter in front of Abbyville's Post Office. The American flag flapped prominently behind her.

"The people of this town certainly hope the government makes a thorough investigation of these people in the *New Hope* Settlement, and soon."

Hioto Mishito angrily shut off the TV. "Sounds like they're afraid of this *New Hope* Settlement."

"Of course they are," Gunther Klein, VP, European Economic Community Operations, snorted. "Making children do chores, teaching them to believe in God, respect authority: it sounds like these people might have hit on something that works. The government is more afraid of people who successfully discipline their children than anything else."

"They're doing a lot better than we are with 300 adults on the Moon," sighed Enrico Sanchez, VP South American Operations.

"And their job is a lot more difficult than yours," added Mrs. Mishito with a wry smile.

*****

The sun shone brightly through the window of the LMC boardroom.

"Well, gentlemen," said Mr. Solte, "I'm hoping for a progress report on the proposal to replace the miners with family units."

"In order to get this done ASAP," said the VP of Human Resources, "we need to be able to do a background check as a group."

"How do you plan to do that?" asked Mr. Solte. "Do you have such a group in mind?"

"No," admitted the Human Resources VP.

"I might have an idea," said Enrico Sanchez, "but let me check it out first."

"Does anyone else have anything to suggest?" asked Mr. Solte.

"We would need a minimum of six weeks for background checks," said the VP of Human Resources. "Whoever we pick."

"There are always alternatives," said Truman Solte. "We simply have to find the best one."

"There might be an alternate way of gathering the information, but I don't think that we'll be able to hire anyone without a full check," said the VP of Human Resources.

"As I said," said Mr. Solte, "We have to find the best alternative. Meeting adjourned."

Truman Solte left first and other board members began to file out. Hioto Mishito, Enrico Sanchez, and Gunther Klein remained behind.

Enrico spoke first. "Remember that special report on

those religious people up north?"

"No," said Gunther. "I - Oh, yes, I remember. You thinking of proposing them to Solte?"

"If the government is investigating them," said Enrico, "it'll be easy to get background information. They're already cooperating with us in the removal operation."

"Are you aware," said Hioto, "that there are quite a few other members of this group still living back at the place they came from?"

"No," said Enrico, "I wasn't."

"The powers that be are giving them a rough time," said Hioto, "closing their churches, emptying their bank accounts. Maybe they're looking for a way out."

"At least we can check," said Gunther. "They could be such religious nuts that they're useless to us."

"I hope not," said Enrico. "We need someone fast, or we're sunk."

"Don't put too much faith in this," said Gunther. "It's likely not going to pan out into anything."

*****

The staging area on the Earth satellite, LMC-I, was large enough to be mistaken for somewhere Earthside. The military units began transferring equipment as soon as the officers finished the paperwork. The well-organized soldiers would only half fill the recently arrived transport on its return trip to LMC-II and the Moon colony.

"Excuse me, Colonel," said the on duty radio operator, "but I think you'll want to hear this incoming communication."

The LMC operator, a tall, dark-haired woman with a nametag that read Kelly, took off her headphones and turned up the speaker volume. A burst of static jumbled with various unrecognizable loud noises and shouting, burst from the speaker.

"Can anybody hear me?" a man's voice crackled over

the din. "This is LMC Moon Base. We've got a major emergency here!"

"Moon Base, we are having difficulty receiving you," said Kelly. Static was the only response. Kelly repeated her message three more times. She changed frequencies.

"LMC-II," asked Kelly, "did you receive a distress call from the surface?"

"Yes, LMC-I," came a new voice. "The colony reports shuttles disabled, life support damaged, some areas of the facility completely inaccessible. The shuttle bay doors refuse to open, so we're unable to evacuate anyone."

The Colonel keyed the mike. "Are the other entrances to the LMC operational?"

"Affirmative, LMC-I," replied the voice. "But both of the shuttles with docking couplers are down there, so we cannot use them."

"So," said the Colonel, "this has turned into a rescue operation. We've got the equipment and we can retrain in transit."

"Sir," said Kelly, "we're a week away. If life support is out, there may not be anyone to rescue."

"We'll do what we can," said the Colonel. "Load up double time, men."

*****

The winter skies at *New Hope* Settlement found people desperately storing seeds, berries and whatever grains they could find. A homemade forge roared in the center compound, but the tools produced were small because there was little metal to work with.

John Winthrop, Anne, Alice and Theo hurried around to stop the frantic activity and bring the adults together.

"Friends," John called out. "Friends! We need to pray."

The people gathered around John and many knelt. Men removed their hats. Anne gripped John's hand tightly.

"Lord God," prayed John, "we came here seeking a country; a place to worship You in Spirit and in Truth. We are discouraged, and it seems we have no hope. Our tools are worn out, our supplies are exhausted, winter is almost here -- Lord, remember our frailty. Support us with Your mighty arm. Deliver us from those who persecute us and steal from us the means to feed our children and build our homes. Free us to serve You."

As John finished praying, a single-engine airplane could be heard landing nearby. The children joined their parents. When the prayer stopped everyone stood, looking around anxiously.

"That didn't sound like an angel of deliverance," said John. "Take the women and children inside. This probably means more trouble."

"Whatever it means, we're going to face it with you, John," said a woman in back.

"All right, keep praying," John suggested. Anne and Elder Jenkins split the men and women into groups, some beneath the washhouse lean-to, some under the smokehouse canopy. They returned to earnest prayer and did not even look up as half a dozen men wearing expensive business suits emerged from the edge of the woods and approached the tiny circle of huts.

John Winthrop and Adolphus walked toward the newcomers, meeting them about 20 meters past *New Hope*'s outermost home.

"Is there someone here named John Winthrop?" asked Enrico Sanchez.

"That's me," said John.

"Sir, my name is Enrico Sanchez and I represent the Lunar Mining Company. Perhaps you've heard of us?"

"Well ... I knew there was such a thing. We've been sort of out of touch. You're not from the government?"

"No, sir. We've come to let you know about a proposal that's being investigated to put family groups into the mining operations on the Moon. This involves a certain degree of technical ability, some knowledge of farming techniques -- there are a variety of skills needed for the operation."

"Families ... on the Moon?" echoed Adolphus.

"With your permission, Mr. Winthrop," said Gunther Klein, "we'd like to carry out background checks on the folks in your settlement."

"For what purpose?" asked John Winthrop.

"This isn't an offer of employment, you understand," said Enrico. "Like I said, we have to make these inquiries, but we are looking for a large number of stable, responsible people to fill positions in our lunar facility. Families. People who are self-sufficient, willing to work."

"You're considering us for these mining jobs?" asked John Winthrop.

"Mining is the general term we use," said Hioto. "But the actual mining is automated. It's just too dangerous. We produce a lot of things on the Moon. Food, optical equipment, computer components, but our major products are the drugs RD-777 and RD27851... May we proceed with the investigations?"

"I suppose we should talk it over first," said Jon Winthrop. "Do you mind?"

"Of course not," said Enrico. "We'll stay here."

John and Adolphus trudged back to the other settlers. Everyone gathered by their unfinished church building and looked uneasily at the shivering businessmen.

"The government's pretty desperate, sending agents all the way out here to arrest us," said one man with a weak chuckle. "They don't look like the ATF."

"IRS Special Forces," grinned Anne Winthrop, holding William close.

"A tax evasion strike team. That's it." Several people laughed, but nervously.

"No," said John, "that's what I thought at first. They're representatives of the Lunar Mining Company. They say that their board wants to put families up on the Moon."

"I remember hearing that they had some kind of trouble at their plant up there and needed more workers," George Raymond said.

"They want us to go live on the Moon?" said someone else.

"Things are bad here, but..." Adolphus trailed off.

"What kind of trouble did they have with the other workers?" asked Craig Newcombe.

"Pay dispute," said John Winthrop, after struggling to recall the story from the last newspaper he had read. "The workers -- um -- I think they left because they felt they weren't making enough money."

"I thought it was a strike," someone ventured.

"Do we really want to be strikebreakers on the Moon?" asked Elder Jenkins. "Sounds a little dangerous for the women and children."

"More dangerous than freezing and starving here this winter?" asked Diane Newcombe.

"This isn't really an offer, yet," John admonished. "They just want to know if they can do background checks."

"Do they know we're in trouble with the government?" asked another voice from the back. John looked into the eyes of his son Theo as he stepped into view. He glanced again at the men standing patiently at the edge of the clearing.

"I'd be surprised if they don't," answered John. "The press has been telling everyone what freaks we are, and how they want the government to do something about us."

"But why us?" Alice asked.

"Because it's a crazy idea and they know we've got to try something. They think that we might be desperate enough to go along with them," Adolphus exclaimed.

John Winthrop raised his hands to stop the rising disagreements. "I think we should tell them to go ahead. It doesn't mean they'll approve us, or that we have to go. We can pray about it; consider it in the meantime."

"Why not?" shrugged George.

Winthrop gestured to the LMC men and they came over to the settlers.

"Yes," said John Winthrop, "you can do whatever checking on us you feel is necessary. I hope you understand, though, that you may find certain information that isn't entirely accurate: delinquent tax charges and civil disobedience sorts of things."

"Well, sir," said Enrico, "some preliminary checking was done before we came, and I think there are folks who are able to put all the data in the proper perspective."

"Thank you," said John, "and if you need more people, please allow me to suggest some other brothers and sisters in Christ that are being persecuted. I could give you names and addresses."

"I'm sure that'd be helpful, sir," said Enrico. "Thank you for your cooperation. We'll be in touch with you soon."

Seven

The 5,000-kilo shuttle landed next to the antenna array building and a specialized coupler attached. In less than fifteen minutes, the shuttle bay door dematerialized and the first shuttle left for LMC-II.

The rescuers had to force open non-functioning doors, work around several ruined shuttlecrafts, search through wreckage, and avoid the injured and dead being loaded into the remaining shuttles.

Jonathan Newton landed with the initial shuttle, worked feverishly until the entire colony was evacuated. He piloted the last shuttle out, carrying the last of the survivors.

"I know we wanted to make a point, Jon..." groaned Mike Connors, pushing aside the medical corpsman checking his splinted arm, "but I didn't think it would go this far."

"The company's replacing us, Mike," Jon murmured.

"Can't say I blame 'em. But the place is such a wreck that I'm not sure it can be repaired. We can't even get to the agricultural section; the control panel for the nuclear reactor is inaccessible; door controls don't function..."

"Maybe they'll let some of us stay on. The new guys will need help."

"They might shoot us all, too, Jon. I'm not sure we don't deserve it."

"What happened, anyway?"

"Shut up, Mike," said Joe Miller. He apparently had not been injured.

"You shut up, Joe," snarled Mike. "I'm sick about this. Someone closed the secondary steam valve to the main generator and when it blew, the steam took out the auxiliary power system. We had to use every battery we had."

"What do you know about it, Joe?" Jon demanded.

"Nothing! It was just another accident."

"Sure it was," said Jon. "Who closed the valve, Joe?"

"What difference does it make now? Nobody was supposed to get hurt. That part was an accident."

"Tell me who did it." Jon persisted.

"You're a traitor, Jon Newton," said Joe. "You'd tell the company to make yourself look good, wouldn't you?"

Jon Newton never took his eyes off his controls, but his voice commanded the attention of everyone in the shuttle. "Who's a traitor? The guy who almost killed everybody in the colony, I'd say. Money's not worth killing people over. I wish we'd never started all this."

"Jon," said Mike, "maybe we could make up for this if we try to help the new people."

"They can't just fire us!" squalled Joe. "We have a contract!"

"I think it's been slightly violated, Joe," snorted Jon. "And we've already been fired. These troops came to clean us out. It was just incidental that they happened to be here to help rescue you. I hear tell they want to put families up here. That should be interesting."

"Families?" asked Mike. "Guys bringing their wives and kids up here?"

"We'll see about that," grunted Joe.

*****

Enrico Sanchez stood before the LMC board with only two note cards. Everyone had arrived at least ten minutes earlier. They watched the digital clock change to 9:00 am EST. Sanchez cleared his throat and began.

"In view of our desperate circumstances, Mr. Solte, I'd like to propose a group of families we've been investigating. They have a rather strong religious code which some people have called fanatical, but our

54

background checks reveal that they are honest, hard-working and self-sacrificing, with a variety of skills that should be useful in the colony."

"How many families are involved here?" asked Mr. Solte.

"There are about 300 men," Mr. Sanchez replied, "plus their wives and children, of course. Some have rather large families. The total number of people is around 1000."

"With everything up and running," noted the VP of Human Resources, "the current facilities were designed to handle about twice that many adults. The individual living quarters, however, would have to be modified to accommodate all of these families."

"A lot will have to be done just to make the colony habitable again," said Mr. Sanchez. "Now, these people haven't agreed to any proposal yet, and we haven't really made one. However, Human Resources reports that background checks will be completed on them by the end of the week, thanks to the fact that the government has been investigating them for tax evasion. Right now, it's all we've got."

"We do have one other thing," said the VP of Human Resources. "A few of the ousted miners have asked to be considered as trainers for whomever we put up there as replacements. They're willing to accept whatever terms we dictate, and to be considered temporary workers. A number of the men have expressed regret about what happened. And our investigations indicate that they can be trusted. It seems that the serious sabotage was done by a very few miners."

"It's a little late for regrets," said Mr. Solte. "But I suppose we'll have to have someone up there. Check these volunteers out thoroughly. And I want a little broader searching done for family units. We don't have to limit ourselves to these people if there's some question as to their suitability."

*****

All the miners disembarked from three transports and mingled in the corridors and staging areas of LMC-I. The first shuttle from Earth arrived a few minutes after the last transport and needed refitting before it could leave for the return flight.

"You know they're replacing us, don't you?" remarked Sam Aleti to the tall black man standing next to him.

"With who?"

"People are saying families."

"They fired everybody?" demanded a thin, gray-haired man.

"I heard there's gonna be some temporary jobs for trainers until the new people know what they're doing," said a heavyset man.

Clay Jones had already concluded that D-20 infractions were no longer important to him and had been expressing his opinions about the company quite steadily throughout the trip.

"They're throwing us out, just like that?" he spat.

"Seems like they've got a right to be mad," Sam reasoned.

"But some guys get to keep their jobs," Clay complained. "The rest of us are out."

"The guys keeping their jobs might be up there 3 months, 6 at the most," Sam retorted. "Look, we went too far. It's over."

"We'll see about that. They just might be willing to take us back, if they can't get anyone else."

Eight

"About sixty men started the application process," announced the VP of Human Resources, "but all have since withdrawn themselves from consideration."

"What reasons did they give for withdrawing?" asked Mr. Solte.

"Sir," continued the VP, "it seems that they suffered various injuries. Most of them won't talk about it, but our investigators have concluded that someone may have put pressure on them to withdraw."

"Would those men really go that far?" asked Gunther Klein.

"It would appear that they have," said the VP of Human Resources, "but there isn't any proof. Some men slipped through the cracks when everyone was brought back and are missing. Unfortunately, among them are men suspected of having been deeply involved in the sabotage and slowdowns."

"We're not giving in to extortion, gentlemen," said Mr. Solte.

"Sir," said Enrico Sanchez, "may I recommend this religious group we discussed before? They're in Alaska -- isolated enough, I believe, that the miners may not be aware of them. And their background check is complete."

"If we can quietly negotiate a contract with them, we may be able to circumvent the miners," said Mr. Mishito.

"What have the background checks turned up?" asked Mr. Solte.

"Sir," said the VP of Human Resources, "they're decent, hardworking, honest, nonviolent religious kooks. Not the sort you'd want as your next-door neighbor, but certainly unlikely to cause more trouble for the colony. The government is prepared to facilitate their removal in exchange for any property they might leave behind. Some kind of back tax thing. I have a complete report with me for anyone interested."

"You gentlemen should be aware," said Mr. Solte, "that there have been some threats of reprisals if we try to restart operations."

"These new people don't need to know about that," said Gunther Klein. "The miners won't be able to reach them once they're off the Earth. Our security can easily prevent any problems up there."

"Very well," said Mr. Solte. "Draw up some sort of agreement ... They probably won't be as productive, and it will cost more to feed all of them ... I hope they learn quickly."

*****

Enrico Sanchez, Gunther Klein, Hioto Mishito and their wives sat near the restaurant's TV monitor, watching the news as they waited for their meal.

"Popular support is growing for the cause of the recently ousted Lunar Mining Company employees," said the perfectly featured petite brunette reporter. "They were removed by military action shortly after a tragic accident claimed several lives and almost destroyed the facility."

The scene cut to a small Italian man with baggy overalls. Someone held a microphone out for him.

"They didn't have a chance. The army charged in and cleaned 'em out."

"All they wanted was more pay," said a policeman exiting his patrol car. "Man, they were risking their lives up there."

"A lot of stuff you buy these days comes from the Moon," said a woman. She was hidden in shadow, so it was difficult to make out anything distinctive. "Now there are shortages everywhere."

The camera cut to a tall black man in a navy suit with a maroon brief case. "Shouldn't the company have negotiated with them? Maybe there's still a way to work something out. That's what democracy's all about."

Six heads swung around as the waiter deftly began placing salads.

"I like that unbiased coverage," said the petite Mrs. Mishito. "No mention of all the sabotage and deliberate slowdowns."

"Or the fact that the destruction of the power plant was no accident," said Mrs. Klein.

"Or the threats and intimidation since the miners came back to Earth," said Enrico. "Well, maybe it'll die down once the new group is in place."

*****

The Winthrop's small cabin was crowded with nearly three dozen men. A number of church members who had not joined the *New Hope* Settlement had flown in for this meeting, their fares paid by the LMC corporation as a gesture of goodwill.

"A wise man is he who listens to counsel," Pastor Earl Collins said. "John, you've talked with these men at length, face to face. We've only dealt with them over the phone."

"Pastor," said John Winthrop, "I wish I thought we had a choice. But the government plans to confiscate your personal property even if you stay and give up your beliefs. And you're losing the battle for your children. They're making heroes out of school counselors and social workers and they backtalk and defy you."

"But we're not making it here, either, Pastor," said a voice from the back. "We can't get supplies, our crops were poor..."

Pastor Collins said, "The Scriptures command us to examine everything carefully. I know that you have spent a lot of time praying and looking into this, John. What do you advise?"

John Winthrop hesitated. He smiled and said firmly, "It's a chance to put our faith on display. If the Lunar Mining Colony isn't a city set on a hill, I don't know what is. I think God is driving us in this direction. Of course it'll be hard. But He will be there with us."

"We've prayed about this, and the congregation voted to do as you advised, John," said Carl Hodges, who had flown in with the pastor.

"You've dealt with these people and explained their offer to us," the pastor said. "Let's trust the Lord and go forward."

"We would be a City on a Hill. Let's close in prayer, gentlemen, and we'll contact the company representatives."

*****

The first shuttle of *New Hope* settlers debarked onto LMC-I amid impolite stares. Children were as novel to the crewmen as LMC-I was to the settlers.

"Welcome to the New World, folks," said a tall man, stepping forward.

Five-year-old Sarah Winthrop looked up at him. She moved past the man and touched a wall gingerly. "Daddy, is this the Moon?"

The satellite crewmembers laughed, breaking off their study of the settlers and moving back to their workstations. The tall man did not withdraw. John Winthrop stepped forward to place himself between Sarah and the stranger. The man put out a huge hand in greeting.

"My name's Jonathan Newton. No, this is LMC-I, the Earth space station," he explained. "The moon isn't quite this close to Earth."

"Of course. That's right, Sarah," her father said. "I'm John Winthrop." He grasped the large hand.

"Like I said, welcome," Jon Newton said awkwardly, returning Winthrop's hearty handshake. "I'm in charge of the training team. We'll have plenty of time for introductions after we board the transports. It'll take a week to get to LMC-II, the lunar satellite. That's when you'll get to see your new home."

"And you'll have to excuse the mess," said Mike Conners, who had also stayed on as a trainer. "It's so hard to get good help these days."

"Well," said Anne, "I didn't plan to sit around looking at the stars, anyway."

"No, ma'am," said Mike, "you won't be doing much of that for a long time to come."

"We'll start training as soon as we're in transit," said Jon Newton. "Don't expect a lot of free time. The colony's in bad shape. Repairs have to be done quickly, and if you get your lessons down, you'll waste less time fixing mistakes. Next we have to get production started. Solte said you were hardworking folks. I sure hope so."

*****

The monitor in the small room was filled with the Moon. LMC-II, clearly visible, was less than an hour distant. Docking procedures were underway. Jon Newton, along with Mike and two other former miners, sat at a small table with half a dozen new men watching the beginning approach to LMC-II.

"I don't want to scare anyone, but we will have to go down first and restart the reactor," said Jon. "The core and primary coolant are undamaged, but we have to shut this valve." He pointed to a diagram. "After that we put more water in the secondary system and bring everything back online. The auxiliary power must be operational before the women and children can come down from LMC-II."

"What if there's radiation leakage?" asked a colonist with Smith printed on his nametag.

"We have radiation suits," said Jon Newton. "Someone will have to go in and repair the problem. He'll have to decontaminate the affected area after that. It's easier and safer than it would be on Earth. We have picked the six of you because you have demonstrated the necessary skills."

"That's not quite the right way to put it," said Mike. "About three dozen men demonstrated the necessary skills. We had to narrow the selection down, so we picked you. It was random. Well sort of."

"Anyway," said Jon, "let me give you your assignments. We're leaving directly from the transport and coupling up to the agricultural entrance. It's the closest to the reactor and we don't even know if we can get through the main hallways. It might be the only way to the reactor."

"We're leaving for the moon immediately?" asked John Winthrop. "But you haven't shown us anything about our space suits."

The miners laughed.

"We don't wear space suits," said Mike. "Too pricey. They're bulky; they're not stylish. Why, imagine wearing something so tacky on the surface of the moon. Positively gauche."

"All true," said Jon Newton, "but the real reason is that we cannot afford to vent the air. It's too valuable."

Nine

The reactor startup was uneventful. The radiation monitors showed that radiation suits were unnecessary. Water was transported down and auxiliary power was operational in less than six hours. Jon assembled his team back in the shuttle.

"The tests say that we could start up the mains immediately," said Jon Newton, "but I don't fully trust the testing equipment. A thorough diagnostic is going to take some time, since I have to divide my time among other priorities. The main shuttle bay is operational. The solar panel arrays are at one hundred per cent. We have enough batteries to replace every single one if we have to. No children until the main is online, but anyone who is willing and able to work can come on down."

"How long before the main is online?" asked Mike.

"Maybe tomorrow, maybe next month," said Jon. "Every piece of equipment that has anything to do with the reactor is getting a level one diagnostic first. We're not taking any chances."

"Does this place always smell like this?" asked Carl Hodges.

"Life Support has only been fully operational for three hours," said Mike. "It'll smell like a rose tomorrow."

"At least it'll smell like it always did," grunted Jon. "Since you can't get to the main complex area from here, you might as well come with me back to LMC-II."

*****

"Lord," prayed John Winthrop as he worked on a control panel in the reactor area. "You sent us here. Now

You help me fix this thing."

Jon Newton, hearing the prayer, walked into the room. He stepped over to the panel, looked at an instrument, and flipped a switch.

"The Lord must've heard you, Winthrop. It's working fine now."

"It is?"

"Yeah," said Jon Newton, "and it's the only one that's been successfully repaired so far. That's how come you didn't realize it was working, because we haven't got a working one to show you. Good job, Mr. Technician."

"I had a good teacher."

"You mean God, I suppose," said Jon Newton. He looked around and noticed that they were alone.

"I mean you, of course. All of you men. You've been very good to us, and we're grateful."

"You guys sure got a funny way of looking at things. We work you eighteen hours a day, yell at you for every little mistake, threaten to bounce you into orbit, complain about your wives' cooking ... and you thank us."

"You've had some hard lessons to communicate to some thick-headed people. I wish we were as good at teaching you."

"Whoa, now. I smell a sermon coming. I thought we had an agreement about that."

"You said you didn't want to hear about the Lord. I remember. But just now you said you didn't understand our attitude. I was trying to explain it."

"Touché, John. So God makes you put up with obnoxious people and lousy living conditions. And you still say you love Him?"

"This life only lasts a little while, Mr. Newton. I'll have all of eternity to forget about this. But God will remember what I've done here, or what I haven't done. I'm trying to earn a good reputation in Heaven. You know, a 'Well done, thou good and faithful servant. Enter into the joy of thy Lord.'"

"How come we always get told to take life one day at

a time, live for the moment, and … oh, I won't do a beer commercial. You're saying you don't consider this life important -- you just look forward to dying?"

"I look forward to eternity. We are strangers and pilgrims, seeking a place where we can fear God and enjoy Him forever."

"And you all feel the same way?"

"Each person must make a decision to follow God. It isn't belonging to a group or following what others are doing. The Lord Jesus Christ takes up residence within us. We are changed, and part of that is seeking to be more like Him every day."

"And since the Lord lived," said Anne Winthrop, coming up so quietly that neither man had noticed her arrival, "and died working hard and pouring Himself out into the lives of others, we try to do the same. We know that because He lives, we shall live also. Now, are you fellows ready for supper?"

"Not ration tins again, please," moaned Jon Newton.

"Some ladies and older children surveyed the greenhouses today," said Anne. "We're having salad with our ration tins, at least. There's quite a lot of produce that wasn't destroyed."

"The greenhouses?" said Newton. "I thought that passageway was still buried in the rubble."

"Well," said Anne, "it did take us most of the day to clear it out. But the damage inside wasn't as bad as you fellows thought."

"You people are incredible," said Newton. "A bunch of women and kids … Okay, okay, I get the message. Let's go eat."

*****

The bar in the rec room had been torn down and a large monitor displaying Earth broadcasts had taken its place. Children played Ping-Pong, tag or just ran around while adults watched the news.

"Demonstrations have continued outside the main

65

headquarters of the Lunar Mining Company," said the reporter.

"Today thousands carried placards denouncing what is termed the unfair treatment of miners by company officials."

The reporter stood outside the headquarters building, a large American flag making most of the background. She turned slightly to her left and the camera cut to a close-up of protesters carefully arranged to look like a large crowd. Despite artful camera work it was obvious that there were very few protesters. One man stepped up to the microphone. The words, "Miners' spokesperson," were superimposed above him. If Jon Newton had been in the room, he would have recognized Joe Miller.

"People haven't forgotten what happened up there. We took the risks. That accident proves how dangerous it was. But they just threw us out."

"It wasn't so long ago that company officials took advantage of a tragic accident to forcibly evacuate and fire the original mining crews," said a voiceover. "Vigils have been held in memory of the miners who died in this tragedy. But those who lived to tell the tale are angry with company officials."

The camera cut to several close-ups before cutting back to the 'spokesperson.'

"They just replaced us with some untrained religious fanatics," Joe shouted. "Who knows what's going on up there? People are counting on production being restored, but without trained personnel with the necessary skills, I don't see how it's possible. The company's deceiving everybody."

*****

More than a dozen men worked on the 50,000-kilo shuttle in the lower shuttle bay. The main bay was almost undamaged, but the batteries had been stripped or jumped, causing extensive electrical damage. All of the smaller shuttles were operational, but the largest shuttle, since it had the most powerful electrical system, had been cannibalized the most.

"If we can get this shuttle up and running," said Jon Newton, "we'll be ready to start shipping when the last of the products are packaged. You sure your ladies' aid society can get those vegetables packaged in time?"

"I have complete faith in them," said John Winthrop. "They'll be ready when we are. Just one more --"

Winthrop collapsed, scattering tools. Several men ran over to him.

"Get the doctor!" shouted Mike, the first man to reach him.

*****

Anne tucked the sheets closer around her husband. John Winthrop awoke with a start. Anne touched a button and Jon Newton, the doctor and several elders entered the room. Winthrop slowly sat up.

"John," said the doctor, "do you know what this is?"

"A radiation card?" said Winthrop weakly.

"Your radiation card," said the doctor. "You've been exposed to over 100 rads."

"How?" asked John.

"The radiation meters read safe when you were working in the reactor room," said Jon Newton, "but they were malfunctioning. We didn't know that until we retraced your footsteps. No one else was in there long enough to be permanently affected."

"You, however, have one to two weeks to live," said the doctor.

Everyone except Anne took a few steps away from the bed. John Winthrop motioned to Jon Newton to come closer.

"What if you were here?" asked Winthrop. "That would worry me."

"John," said Jon. "Not now. Not a sermon."

"This is my last chance, Jon. But you don't need a

sermon. You've heard enough to know what you need to do." John reached for his wife's hand.

"Anne, I love you," said John. "I'll be waiting."

"I love you, too, John." Anne kissed him on the forehead. Jon Newton again tried to slip away, but John Winthrop snagged his arm and held on.

"Try to do something with this fellow, will you?" he said to Anne. "Something could happen to him. He's not ready."

*****

"I can almost hear it," said Jon Newton. The rec room seemed hollow and empty without children. The monitors displayed the eternal view of Earth from the camera mounted in the antenna array dome. The lights, dimmed since 2300 hours EST, left any remaining adults in pockets of privacy.

"Hear what?" asked Anne Winthrop. Her own voice seemed hollow in the spacious, vacant hall.

"That *Well done, thou good and faithful servant,*" said Jon.

"I think I can too," said Anne.

"I want to hear it myself, someday," said Jon.

"There's nothing to keep you from it except yourself," said Anne.

"Was it my fault?" asked Jon.

"Of course not. It was an accident. You men are always so careful about the safety rules. It's --"

"I don't mean that. Did God kill John to shake me up? You know, to get my attention."

"God has two purposes in everything: to bring glory to Himself and to bring man to Himself. He uses all sorts of methods to accomplish those purposes."

"I was responsible for your husband's safety. So now there's a widow with five children that I'm responsible for."

"God's responsible for us, Jon. He has been for many years. But if you think God has a message for you, perhaps you'd better listen."

*****

People crowded the LMC COM center, watching the monitor view of the 50,000 kilo shuttle completing docking with LMC-II. Suddenly the image switched to an Earth-based TV news program. Shots of burning buildings and milling crowds flickered across the screen. Reporters chased harried rescue workers with microphones and cameras in spite of police officers that tried to keep them back. A breathless reporter stepped up into the shot.

"Protesters lashing out against domino-effect shortages in most areas of the economy teamed up with ousted employees of the Lunar Mining Company in violent confrontations at LMC sites around the world," he said. The camera cut to more footage of the disaster, and the reporter's voice continued in the background. "In spite of heavy security, miners and their supporters stormed buildings, looting and burning. It is uncertain at this time how many LMC officials have been killed, since rescue workers have been unable to enter the rioter-held buildings."

Images of gutted buildings; angry mobs, fires, emergency crews and body bags filled the screen.

"That's why our message that we were ready to transport never got an answer," said Jon Newton, watching from near the back of the room. Anne Winthrop stood near him. "After all this work to start filling a transport, there's no one to receive it."

"Oh, Jon, what will we do?"

"I guess it's time to pray," said Jon. "No, that's not how your husband would have said it. It's time to pray."

"That sounds strange," said Anne, "coming from you."

"Well," said Jon, "you gave me John's Bible, and I sort of felt obligated to read it. You know that place in Luke where it says, *'Weren't our hearts burning within us, while He was speaking to us on the road, and while He was explaining the Scriptures to us?'*

"I would read, and I would imagine how John might explain it to me. I couldn't get him out of my thoughts. But that verse is talking about Jesus Christ, actually. So I realized I had to let the Lord teach me, but that He needed to be living in me to do that. So I asked Him."

"What do you mean?" asked Anne.

"I mean, I asked the Lord to forgive my sins," said Jon. "I repented and asked Him to save me. And He did."

"Oh, that's wonderful!" said Anne. She stretched up and hugged him.

"I guess John was shouting 'Hallelujah' through the pearly gates, after all the times he tried to convert me. Say, Mrs. Winthrop, you can let go now."

Anne stepped back, embarrassed, and said, "I'm so happy for you, Jon."

"Maybe what's going on down on Earth isn't all that serious," said Jon. "The news people tend to get carried away. At least, by the time the transports are full, we can hope the company will be up and running again."

*****

Jon Newton sat in the small control room on LMC-II watching a monitor with the on-duty radioman. The first transport, *War-Horse*, filled with production from the new colonists of the Lunar Mining Colony, fired her thrusters for LMC-I. Mike Connors, along with the other trainers, were aboard, headed back to Earth.

"Guess you're the official Company Rep now," said Mikelovich.

"Huh?" said Newton.

Mikelovich zoomed the camera in on *War-Horse*. "You're the only one of the original miners left now. How long are you going to stick around?"

"Oh ... I ... don't know," said Newton. "I guess a little while longer. Those people kind of ... make you feel at home. We still can't communicate with Earth Base?"

"No," returned Mikelovich, "and that's really strange. You'd think they'd have fixed up something by now. There's just the one-way TV signals and things like that. We're really out of touch. I hope this doesn't mean paychecks will be late."

The monitor switched to a shot of Anne Winthrop.

"Hello, LMC-II," said Anne. "This is Moon Base."

"Wow," said Mikelovich, "she's not bad looking for a middle-aged lady."

Jon cuffed him.

"Just don't you forget she is a lady," said Jon. "And besides, she's got five kids."

"Five kids! Man, I'm not that attracted to older women!"

"Good. Let's just keep it that way. Afternoon, Mrs. Winthrop. What can we do for you?"

"Just wanted to confirm that the transport is on its way," said Anne.

"Yes, Ma'am," said Jon, "with its belly full of goodies for Earth. If we do all right with this shipment, we'll be back on track."

"Will you be coming for supper, Mr. Newton?" asked Anne.

"Oh, yes, ma'am," said Jon. "At my place I'm still eating out of ration tins."

"Hmm. And leaving them lying around, I'll bet. Maybe I'll break into your quarters and tidy up a little before you get back."

"Oh, no, Mrs. Winthrop, don't trouble yourself--" The monitor cut back to the *War-Horse* and Mikelovich had to zoom again.

"Five kids doesn't seem to bother you much," said Mikelovich. "You ain't thinking of marrying after all these years, are you, Newton?"

"If she really does get in to my room, I doubt if there's much chance of it. I'd better get back."

*****

For the next week, the colonists worked to fill a second transport, which left on schedule. The colonists gathered in the rec room to watch the second transport leave LMC-II.

"Now hear this, everybody," said a voice over the speakers. "The first transport has arrived safely at LMC-I. Looks like we're going to make this thing work. God be praised."

The colonists cheered, hugged and roughhoused for several minutes before going back to work. Anne Winthrop walked by the radio room and saw Jon Newton watching an Earth news broadcast.

"As if the Lunar Mining Colony had yet to atone for its sins against ousted miners," said a woman's voice, "an event has taken place that will surely spell the end of the company's speculative venture in space."

The newscast ran footage captured from the camera of the *War-Horse*. It showed the docking clamps of the LMC-I locking on. An instant later LMC-I began to shake violently and the rock steady picture from the *War-Horse* began to sway. Pieces of the LMC-I begin to fly off and the camera went dead.

"Reports indicate," continued the voiceover, "that the low-Earth-orbit satellite known as LMC-I, designed to transfer goods and supplies between Earth and the moon, has been completely destroyed in a spectacular explosion. There are also unconfirmed rumors that a transport from the moon had arrived at the satellite just before the disaster, and may also have been destroyed. Experts believe that the footage you are now seeing came from a camera on that transport.

"There have been no communications from the lunar base in months, and this transport may have represented the first shipments of moon products since the explosion that disabled the facility. Products from the moon could have been used to help curb the widespread shortages, and might even have prevented the rioting and destruction here on Earth. It is assumed that no one could have survived this terrible mishap."

The monitor showed wide-scale rioting and destruction.

"No rescue attempts are even planned, with the rioting and chaos still reigning here on Earth as a result of critical shortages of Moon supplies. The world has gone mad, ladies and gentlemen.

"Some say the Lunar Mining Colony was Earth's only hope. But of course we have confirmation that no upper-level personnel in the company remain alive, and communication with the Moon has been cut off since the rioting began, so we have no real hope that things can be set right again. Indeed, it is speculated that those who presently inhabit the moon colony may have deliberately severed ties with Earth."

"That's a likely story," said Newton. "But it has the same effect."

"What do you mean?" asked Anne.

"I'd rather not explain it twelve hundred times," said Jon. "We need to have a meeting. Let's be in the rec room in half an hour. Spread the word."

Ten

In the LMC rec room, Jon Newton stood on the same platform from which Liz had vainly attempted to calm the miners over three months earlier. This time the room was completely silent and Jon had everyone's full attention.

"Lots of rumors have been flying around already," called out Jon Newton, "and probably have been since this riot trouble on Earth first came up. Now, you've all heard that LMC-I, the Earth's satellite, has been destroyed. Some of you may have already figured out what that means, but I'm going to explain it so everyone will understand that no rumors you've heard can be as bad as what's really happened."

Jon pointed to a monitor that showed, in wire frame, the LMC-I with a transport docked to it.

"Here's what LMC-I looked like. It was similar to LMC-II, though much larger. You're all a little more familiar with that one. And these are the transports we use to ferry things back and forth between the satellites. Now, I don't want to get technical, but the way these transports operate is to attach themselves to the space station's cargo bays with a specialized docking device. It was developed exclusively for LMC and there are no others in existence on Earth as far as I, or any of the men I've consulted with, know. These docking devices are not complicated, but it will take some time to manufacture new ones. What this means is that we can fill transports from now till Christmas, but there's no way to get the cargo to Earth."

"What do you mean?" demanded Carl Hodges. "Can't

they send ships straight up from Earth to receive cargo?"

"Yes, but it's difficult to imagine the problems," said Jon. "Nothing that we manufacture is designed for a vacuum. Without some type of docking device, all cargo would have to be transported through space. Even if we could change the packaging, transporting across a vacuum would require equipment we do not have. And if we had the equipment, one simple transfer would take weeks. Without a satellite station to dock with, those transports are useless."

"There are companies on Earth that transport things into space with heavy launch vehicles," suggested James Andrews. "Not one of them can be used?"

"I don't know," said Jon, shaking his head. "They might be able to modify their docking devices, but I just don't know how."

"We counted on getting supplies in the return trip of that transport that was destroyed, didn't we?" Elder Leon Asahi asked.

"Yes," said Jon. "Stores are very low, as I'm sure many of you know. We have no way of getting supplies here either. For the short term that isn't very serious. We're entering a daylight cycle at the end of next week, so we could, if we had to, shut down the reactor, run on auxiliary power from the solar panels, purify and use the water from the steam generators. With careful conservation we could get by for about a year without any additional food or water. If nothing breaks. Medical supplies are much lower, fuel for the shuttles is about a two-month supply, but oxygen won't last that long."

"Mr. Newton, may I make a suggestion?" ventured nineteen-year-old Alice Winthrop.

"What's on your mind, Miss Winthrop?" asked Jon. He could not help the strange feeling that, when he looked at Alice, he saw John Winthrop's eyes looking out of a younger version of Anne Winthrop's body. Jon did not know the Winthrop children well, but his few encounters with them had convinced him of one thing.

Even if John Winthrop had left no other legacy, he had a monument in his five children, who from William on up impressed him with their self-discipline and maturity.

"Sir," she started slowly, "it seems to me that what we need is to establish contact with the company's creditors. It would be in their best interest to allow us to assume the company's debts -- to become the company ourselves. It seems there aren't any Earth-side representatives. We could take responsibility for its financial obligations."

"Miss Winthrop," said Jon, "how do you propose that we pay the company's debts?"

"Sir," continued Alice, "I'm taking economics right now, and my mother and I figured out that covering a default by LMC on its Earthside loans would bankrupt scores of companies -- maybe whole countries. If they knew that we've restored full production--"

"That may be a slight exaggeration--" said Jon.

"We will be at full production by the end of the week, Mr. Newton," insisted Alice, not at all hesitant now. "I've checked all the records. As I was saying, we can inform them that we've restored the colony to full output. We'll say that we're going to strive to exceed the goals set by the board of directors. It's likely that these creditors would work hard to find a way to receive the cargo. I believe they'd manage to outfit heavy launch vehicles with the proper docking devices."

"Miss Winthrop," said Jon, smiling, "I admire your progress in the area of economics, but your grasp of engineering is somewhat lacking. They'd need half a dozen of the largest known heavy launch vehicles from Earth to receive one load from our transports. Besides, the records of the Colony's creditors were kept Earthside. They may be destroyed, for all we know."

"Mr. Newton," asserted Alice, "I have a listing of the largest corporations in the world in my economics curriculum. I'll take it upon myself to contact them and negotiate the arrangements. You can have men standing by to give technical advice as needed for the docking arrangements, and cargoes ready to ship when the heavy launch vehicles are ready to receive."

Jon stopped smiling and everyone strained to listen. He chose his next words carefully. "Do you have a proposal to restore radio contact with Earth, Miss Winthrop? That's a rather crucial part of your plan."

"Mr. Newton," fifteen-year-old Theo Winthrop spoke up. "I believe our transmitter was damaged by a solar flare. If that's true, most likely the problem is with the link-up on LMC-II and the low wattage equipment here is functioning properly."

Jon smiled and said, "Well, now, do Sarah, Brad and Willie have anything to contribute?" Most people laughed, a little too loud. "All right, you two. You have free reign to pursue the projects you've proposed. Being that we're short on options, I don't see the harm in your trying. If no one else has anything to propose, this meeting's adjourned. Let's all go back to work."

*****

The Winthrop family had just sat down to dinner. Anne Winthrop nodded to Theo and he opened his mouth to pray. A heavy knock sounded on the door of their quarters. Anne Winthrop opened it and Jon Newton burst in.

"Theo, you were right about the solar flare hit," said Jon Newton. "The LMC-II transmitter is repaired. As soon as you can repair the damage to the base transmitter, we should be on line again."

Theo jumped up. "Can I go now, mom?" he asked excitedly. "I'm not that hungry. This is more important."

Jon Winthrop suddenly seemed to realize where he was. He looked uneasily around at Anne and the other children, all of them staring at him.

"Pardon me, Mrs. Winthrop," he apologized. "I didn't mean to intrude. After dinner's fine, Theo. Excuse me." he backed toward the door.

"Please stay and have dinner with us, Mr. Newton," Anne said quickly. "Theo can go with you as soon as we've finished."

Jon opened his mouth to try to form a polite refusal. He had eaten with the Winthrops before, but there had always been other people beside just himself.

This was John Winthrop's family -- the wife and children of the man for whose death he still felt responsible. He remembered how he had tried to make himself responsible for them -- and how Anne Winthrop had quietly told him they didn't need him. Or had she really meant it that way?

He looked around again. Alice rose quickly and helped her mother as she added a few items to the table to stretch the meal.

"Mr. New-Jon," Willie said with a wide smile. "Eat supper with us?"

"Will, I've told you a million times, it's Mr. Newton," Theo grunted.

"Please stay, Mr. Newton," Sarah said soberly. "My daddy is in Heaven, so there's plenty of room."

Jon paled and glanced at Anne as she brushed close by him with a bowl of salad. She touched his arm and smiled warmly.

"John left room for you, Mr. Newton," Anne reassured him. "He'd want you to stay. And so do we."

"Well..." Jon suddenly realized that he wanted to stay, very much. So he sat down.

*****

Alice sat on a stool in front of the reassembled console in the radio room. Theo finished soldering, poked his head out from under the console, looked up and nodded.

"Magnum Corporation, this is the Lunar Mining Colony. Do you read me?" asked Alice.

"This is a restricted frequency," crackled a voice. "Please identify yourself."

"I've been authorized by the director of operations here on the Lunar Mining Colony as legal representative of the company," said Alice. "We are prepared to make an offer."

"Please identify yourself," repeated the voice.

Alice took a deep breath and spoke louder. "I'm Alice Winthrop, I live on the Lunar Mining Colony and I've been authorized to make you an offer."

"Please transmit your identification code," came the voice again.

Alice suddenly understood. She poked her brother, who had gone back under the console, with a foot. "Theo, go find out what our identification code is. Hurry!"

Theo scrambled out and quickly returned with his mother and a thick book.

"Mom," said Alice, "maybe you should talk to them this time. I guess I just don't sound old enough."

Theo flipped through pages of code.

"Trust in the Lord for just the right words, Alice. You explained your ideas quite clearly to the assembly. Now you just have to say the same thing to a stranger."

Theo pushed in beside Alice and pressed some switches. "Contact established," he shouted. "Code being transmitted."

"We are receiving you, Lunar Mining Colony." A strong male voice had taken the place of the Magnum operator. "Good to know you're still alive up there. This is Emerald Corporation CEO Lance Arden. We're a holding company for Magnum Corp. How can we help you?"

"Mr. Arden," said Alice, "I have a proposal to make to you on behalf of the LMC. We are preparing to ship a transport of goods to Earth in a few days. What we need are specially fitted heavy transport vehicles that can dock with our transports. Can you make modifications in your equipment to accommodate us?"

*****

The main shuttle bay evacuated as the 50,000-kilo

shuttle sealed her hatches and moved into position to be hydraulically lifted to the outer shuttle bay.

"Well," said Jon, double-checking the seal to the main bay, "Looks like we're all dressed up with no place to go. The loading of the transport will be completed in a couple of hours, but we need to know what to do with it."

"We send it to Earth, Mr. Newton." Alice and her mother burst into the shuttle bay from com center. "Two companies have agreed to receive shipments from us."

"Whoa!" said Newton. "Understand I'm delighted, but how many vehicles can they send up?"

"They weren't sure, I'm afraid," said Alice. "It may take a long time to unload the transport, but at least we have customers."

"That's the best news I've heard in months," said Jon. "Let's start on the next transport." He grabbed both women in a bear hug before going back to work.

*****

Com center was packed as Jonathan Newton keyed the mike.

"Transport one, *Fighting Bear*, have you reached the rendezvous point yet?"

"That's affirmative, Moon Base," Carl Hodges, pilot of the *Fighting Bear*, replied. "I have a homing signal, but I don't see anything."

"You don't see anything? Nothing at all?"

"That's affirmative, Moon Base. It's a little early, but somebody should -- Wait a minute. There's something -- Yeah. One ship ... Two ships ... three ... four ... Moon Base, you are not going to believe this. There are six heavy launch vehicles out there. They've only got one docking collar, but they have six launches. We'll load the fuel first. At that point it becomes a training exercise. We're going to need as many experienced pilots as we can get. This will take a while. I'll keep you posted. *Fighting Bear* out."

"Six transports!" asked Jon. "That means they can

80

probably unload stuff as fast as we can send it! Get that next transport ready, people. We're in business."

The packed com center erupted into cheers, shouts and clapping. Anne, Theo and Alice hugged each other, crying. Jonathan put his arms around all three of them.

"John would be so proud of you," Jon whispered.

*****

The rec center's lights dimmed as usual at 2300 EST, leaving Jon Newton and Anne Winthrop in private.

"Two months of regular runs without a major problem," said Jon. "We are actually making payments on the company's debts, and we're getting supplies -- things are being run better than they were when this place was crawling with professional technicians and engineers. Production is better than when we had all four transports."

"The Lord has made this a *land flowing with milk and honey,* Jon," said Anne.

"I'm not so sure I'd go that far," said Jon.

"We've found a home, a place where we can serve the Lord, where we're useful and needed ... *Truly the boundary lines have fallen unto us in pleasant places; Indeed, my heritage is beautiful to me.*"

"I always figured the moon was no place for a woman. It's pretty bleak here. Don't you miss the soft breezes and blue skies?"

"Of course. But everyone I love is here. My children are happy and thriving, our fellow believers are growing ... I couldn't be happier."

"Hmm. I was hoping you could be a little happier, Anne."

"I'm not sure what you mean."

"I mean, I know I could be happier. I could be in the middle of a happy, fun-loving crowd of brilliant people who take their God seriously and love each other unselfishly."

"Aren't you?"

"I'm still on the outside at night when I go home to my little cubicle. It's seriously lonely there."

"I see what you mean. So you're saying that there's a specific group you want to get into -- one that you can come home to."

"That's the idea. I know this little group of six that I envy so much. If we had windows in these cans we call homes, I'd be a lost doggie looking in, smearing the glass with my cold wet nose."

"I haven't had the opportunity to take in a stray in a long time, Jon."

"Well, I'd like to give you the opportunity, Anne. Will you please marry me?"

"I've never been able to refuse big sad eyes and a cold wet nose, Jon. Of course I will."

They leaned over and kissed.

*****

The first lunar wedding took place three weeks later. It was a model of simplicity. The reception was held in the main shuttle bay, the only room that could hold everyone.

But what it lacked in formality, it made up in enthusiasm. The euphoria lasted more than two weeks, infecting everyone and, on rare occasions, interrupted work schedules.

Jon and Anne honeymooned in Newton's quarters and afterward moved into the Winthrop's quarters. Jon felt somewhat uncomfortable leading family devotions at first, but he quickly fit in to the routine.

"Every place on which the sole of your foot treads, I have given it to you, just as I spoke to Moses," Jon read, holding the Bible at arm's length because of Will, who snuggled in his lap. *"No man will be able to stand before you all the days of your life. Just as I have been with Moses, I will be with you; I will not fail you or forsake you. Be strong and courageous, for you shall give this people possession of the land which I swore to their*

fathers to give them. Only be strong and very courageous, be careful to do according to all the law which Moses my servant commanded you; do not turn from it to the right or to the left, so that you may have success wherever you go. Joshua One … um … verses here and there."

"Is that God talking, Daddy Jon?" asked Brad.

"It sure is, Brad," asked Theo. "This is our promised land, isn't it, Mom?"

"Yes, darling," said Anne, "I believe it is."

"Is Daddy Jon gonna be just like Joshua, Mommy?" asked Sarah.

"Well, sweetheart," said Anne, "I believe that God will give Daddy Jon just as much courage as he gave Joshua."

"I think God has given us all courage, mom," said Alice. "He's helped us all to change and grow and … learn that we need to work together."

"Time to pray now, daddy!" said Will.

Sojourner

One

"Primary systems for braking thrust to establish parking orbit around Titan have failed. Switching to primary backup controls."

Several seconds passed. Neither the husband nor the wife stirred in the darkness. The computer continued.

"Backup systems for braking thrust to establish parking orbit around Titan have failed. Switching to redundant systems."

"Not again," sighed Michele.

She smiled weakly at Mark. Both jumped out of bed and dressed silently. The stark, straight, barren walls behind them began to glow with an even light. Mark and Michelle Connors were both in their early forties, alike enough to be brother and sister. Taller than average, they both had brown hair and blue eyes. Mark wore a brief beard, and Michele kept her hair long and loose.

"How many times have all the automated systems failed?" asked Michele.

"Fourth time since we left Martian orbit," said Mark.

"But it hasn't failed completely this time. Yet."

"Main redundant system has failed. Switching to reserve redundant system," said the computer.

They grabbed their clothes and hurried into the darkened hallway. Walls began to glow as they ran past. Except for the monitors showing troubleshooting procedures, the control room was dark. It brightened evenly as they entered and sat at their respective control panels.

"We've got a little less than four minutes before we'll have to scrub this approach," said Mark.

"Reserve redundant system has failed," intoned the computer. "Do you want me to scrub this mission and compute a course back to Lunar Base? In twelve minutes, eleven seconds, we will be out of Martian Base contact. I will be unable to verify a new course without their assistance."

"The oxygen's flowing to the firing chambers," said Mark. "It's the methane that's frozen in the lines somewhere. And it must be closer to the core. The only thrusters that will fire are the five now firing."

"Thirty seconds until the close of this window," said the computer.

"I don't like the idea of just the two of us going down there, cut off from everyone," repeated Michele.

"That's the price of being the first," said Mark. "Besides, it really doesn't make any difference. Radio communication is almost four hours round trip."

"I don't want to run into something and not even be able to warn anyone else," said Michele. "If we're going to die, I want our deaths to mean something."

"This isn't a suicide run, Michele. We're not just running away from our debts. We're going to pick up this load of methane and go home. And we could send a message capsule back with complete records in a worst possible case scenario."

"I'm sure the owners of the Cortez and the El Dorado felt the same way," Michele countered.

"The window is closed," said the computer.

"I thought we settled this before we left Mars," said Mark. "If those ships had been manned, they would have at least returned home. Even if we have to abandon the balloon ship, the life pod can get us home without any problems."

"Without any problems? This isn't just everything we own. It's everything your Mom and Dad own and everything my family owns. It's everything a dozen families we've never met own. If this thing isn't full of methane, we might as well not go back. "

A warning buzzer sounded and one point on the wireframe flashed. "Frozen methane," said Mark. "Not 50 meters from the living area. I'm going out there and hit it with a torch. We don't have time to warm up the tunnel. Computer, recalculate parking orbits that would begin braking thrust within the next forty-five minutes and report the four best. Honey, follow me on video."

"Wear a suit. I don't trust those tunnels."

"Computations for parking orbit will take seven minutes," said the computer. "I will not compute orbits that require firing thrusters earlier than I can finish computations."

"Whatever you say, Honey. But this is a nitrogen level. It couldn't be safer."

Mark put on a light suit with feet, gloves and a clear bubble helmet. He pulled on the door, tried again.

"Is that why the door's frozen?"

Without responding, Mark lit a torch, touched the flame to the door and it slid open.

"You're right," said Mark. "Check on the tubing to ensure that nothing else is frozen. Heat up anything that will be moving."

As the door slid closed behind her husband, Michele turned and sat at the control panel. The colored wireframe showed each piece of mining equipment going through test motions.

Mark's voice came over the speaker. "What's the temperature here?"

Michele changed one monitor to watch her husband. Mark was heating the pipe as she called up the sensor readings. "Your suit's external sensor reads minus 31 degrees C," Michele spoke into the keyed mike. "We're radiating too much heat into space."

"Heat leaks," said Mark. "Now we know what we'll be doing on the trip home. I really can think of more interesting things to do for six months than check for heat loss. But this is still way too warm for frozen methane."

"And too close to the lifepod area," said Michele.

"We've got to raise the core temperature," said Mark.

"How much will that cost?"

"Hopefully nothing," said Mark. "If we raise the temperature enough now, we can replace the methane before we leave."

"Only if it's not mixed with too many other things," said Michele.

"We can refine it."

"You can refine it. All we have is a macrofilter for automatic filtration. I'm rather fond of at least a few hours' sleep each day. Hey! Praise the LORD, the methane's flowing."

"I can see it. I'm shutting down and I'll be right in. Get some sort of video on the main thruster."

Michele adjusted the control panel to bring the main thruster into view.

*****

"Warning:" interrupted the Computer, "Titan's upper atmosphere is turbulent and uneven, with variations in uppermost methane levels as much as 20 kilometers. Turbulence could damage methane harvesting equipment."

The door to the life pod area opened and Mark entered.

"I heard," said Mark. "Have all sections of the mining equipment been tested?"

Michele nodded in the affirmative.

"Computations are complete," said the Computer. "Options are listed on monitor C."

"I think," said Michele, "we should take the first option: Wait up until the thrusters fire. After the gravity shifts we can go back to sleep."

"Agreed," said Mark. "We'll be braking continuously for 5 hours, 23 minutes. The shift to head into parking orbit will be 45 degrees. It will only be a ten degree additional shift for the parking orbit. Remember our first

88

shift? The one that threw us on the floor? It was only twelve degrees."

"I don't care if it slaps us out of bed this time," snapped Michele. "I'm not strapping in!"

Mark smiled and took Michele in his arms.

"My my, aren't we a bit testy?"

"I'm sorry," She squeezed and kissed him. "Forgive me, but months of the same thing -- I knew it'd be like this and we don't have any choices, but it's getting to me just the same."

"The LORD has not left us," said Mark.

"I know," said Michele. "But ... well ... there's just nothing we can do out here all alone."

"Now that's not true," returned Mark. "There are some things we can do because we're alone."

"Just wait until we're safely in the parking orbit," said Michele as she pushed away.

"So you think the parking orbit around Titan will be safe?"

Michele smiled. She programmed some course corrections and came back to Mark's arms.

Two

The darkened bedroom tilted with the deep moan of tortured metal. Mark grabbed both Michele and the bed to keep her from being thrown against the wall. The walls began glowing and the bedclothes slid to the floor.

"Parking orbit established and stable. The time is 1930 hours," intoned the computer. "Awaiting further instructions."

Michele and Mark looked at each other. Michele reached over to steady herself against a wall panel. The chronometer showed 2015 when they began to dress.

"Please check to see if my baby sent us anything," asked Michele.

"Our baby is in Junior High," responded Mark, "and he wouldn't talk to you for a week if he heard you say that."

"I'm not going to tell him," said Michele.

Mark walked over and touched a far wall. The blank wall became a large, flat monitor.

"Nothing from anyone," said Mark. "But remember that Andrea's taking finals this week."

Michele walked over to the message board, touched a colored square and a chair came out of the wall. She sat and began checking the messages herself.

"You didn't check the University schedule, did you? Finals don't start until next week. She could have written if she had only thought of us."

Mark smiled. "How many times did you write home when you were in college?"

"Everyone wants their children to turn out better than they did," said Michele. "And this isn't her home.

She's never been on board."

Mark grabbed her from behind and they both giggled.

*****

"Switching to external video," said Michele.

Both Michele and Mark sat in the main control room and watched as the main monitors showed the upper atmosphere of Titan.

"Main suction tube extending," said Mark. "Lord, we need to succeed with this run. Please give us success."

"Amen," said Michele.

"Amen and Amen," said Mark. "I am now switching to monitor. Computer, alert us to any irregularities."

Several monitors shifted to wireframes of the main suction tube extending from the core openings in the bottom of the balloon.

"Suction tube extended fifty percent of length from balloon at twelve point five kilometers," called out Michele.

"Intermittent contact with upper atmosphere," said the computer. "Additional thrusters firing to stabilize parking orbit. Only 27% reserve thruster capacity."

"What does that mean?" asked Michele.

Mark explained, "If Titan's atmosphere creates any more drag on the *Sojourner*, we have an additional 27% of thruster force to counter it. If we use too much thruster force, we pull away from the surface and must recalculate a new parking orbit. Too little thruster force and Titan will pull us in. In that case, we discontinue the suction, pull in the tube, float away from Titan slightly and recalculate the parking orbit. If we are unable to pull in the tube, we jettison the tube. We have two backup tubes. In the worst case scenario, Titan's atmospheric turbulence would pull the *Sojourner* in and we would have to blow out of the top in the lifepod."

"Tube contact with upper atmosphere in 37 seconds," said the computer.

"I don't think the lifepod can keep us warm enough to get home," said Michele.

The scoop, extended its entire twenty-five-kilometer length, stopped moving on the monitor.

"I'm afraid that I agree with you," said Mark.

Contact was made with the methane upper atmosphere and gases began rushing up the transparent tube. The tube, along with the entire balloon ship, began a deep, even, loud resonation.

"How long will we hold together if this keeps up?" asked Michele.

"Not nearly long enough," responded Mark. "Computer! Any damage?"

"This resonance is within design parameters. No known damage."

"We need to design more isolation into the living area," said Mark.

"Methane entering balloon only 50% pure," said the computer. "Macrofilter is able to eliminate 98.4% of all impurities at the expense of 4.8% of the incoming methane."

"We might be jettisoning gases more valuable than methane!" said Michele. "Computer, analysis of major impurities."

A massive jet of gases battered the outside of the suction tube and the resonance became louder and irregular.

"I thought we might lose the tube, but everything seems to be holding together," said Mark.

"Analysis of major impurities outside of my design parameters," said the computer.

Michele slammed the flat of her palm against the control panel. "So how do we fix your design parameters?"

"I have neither the necessary sensors nor the attendant software," said the computer.

"The gas we're jettisoning is freezing and falling back into the atmosphere, causing quite a storm," said Mark.

"This resonance is outside of design parameters," said the computer.

"Raise suction tube," said Mark.

"Suction tube has developed multiple fractures," said the computer. "Suction is discontinued."

The deep throb of an explosion shook the living area as the monitors showed fragments of the tube falling into Titan's atmosphere.

"Suction tube jettisoned," called out Michele.

The tube monitor went dead as the methane storm violently increased. As the tube disconnected from the balloon ship, the living area became quiet.

"From now on we'll have to store the waste gases and jettison them after we raise the tube," said Mark.

The jets of methane from the storm rose to hit the *Sojourner* itself.

"Full thrusters," cried Mark. All thrusters facing Titan fired and the *Sojourner* moved safely away from the increasing methane storm. The grinding metal from the methane hits grew silent as the *Sojourner* moved out of range.

"Maintain this orbit," said Mark. "Computer, cut back thrusters to maintain this distance. How much methane did we bring on board?"

"1.7%," said the computer. "If that rate could be sustained, the balloon could be filled in 2 days, 4.12 hours."

"Damage report," said Michele.

"No known damage," said the computer. "Both remaining suction tubes completely functional."

"Storm activity over Titan?" asked Mark.

"Storms are localized and subsiding," said the computer. "No indication of building storms by infrared activity."

"I need a shower and change of clothes before we go down again," said Michele.

"I think I'll join you," said Mark.

*****

"Computer," asked Mark. "What is the projected storm activity for the next few hours at the suction site?"

"Available indicators show no projected storm activity," responded the computer.

"Thank you, LORD," prayed Mark.

"Lowering suction tube to 50% of total length, 12.5 kilometers," reported Michele.

"Balloon ship *Sojourner* descending," said Mark.

"Contact of suction tube with Titan's upper atmosphere in 10 seconds."

The monitor showed the second suction tube lowering to contact methane gases of Titan's upper atmosphere.

"Contact," Mark called out. "Suction beginning."

"No vibration?" asked Michele.

"There is some resonance," said Mark. "But it's isolated from the living area. It seems that the excessive resonance problem was caused by the gases we jettisoned."

"Praise the Lord," sighed Michele. "Everything else checks out. Why don't you get some sleep? I'll wake you if anything changes."

"Thank you." They kissed. "Computer, how long before we must jettison waste?"

"Nine hours, seventeen minutes if the rate remains constant," said the computer.

"Don't fill the waste area," cautioned Mark. "If I'm not up, wake me about half an hour before it's full and we'll jettison. Before I go down, what's to eat?"

"I picked a couple of pink grapefruit," said Michele. "And made some bread from last week's wheat harvest. The raisins won't be ready until we're ready to leave. You can always eat some more grapes, though."

"Great. Where's the synth-butter?"

"How can you eat that stuff?"

"It's all we've got," shrugged Mark. "And it's better

than nothing."
"You're crazy."
"Had to be to marry you." Mark grabbed Michele.
"Eat and go to sleep. I want some rest too."
"Wait on the Lord and not on me."

Three

Michele walked into the dark bedroom and the walls
began to glow for her.

"Mark? Time to get up. We had a slight rate increase,
so you've only been down for about six hours."

Mark rolled over and smiled at his wife. He reached
under the bed, opened his drawer, and pulled out his
clothes. As he dressed he asked, "What's today's
Scripture?"

"Luke 3, John the Baptist and the genealogy of
Christ. I read it already. You can read it to yourself while
I pull up the suction tube."

"I wish that we had someone like John the Baptist,"
said Mark. "Someone to answer questions like these
people had. All they did was ask and John told them what
to do."

"I thought we were supposed to answer questions,"
said Michele.

"I wish I had the answers," said Mark. "You know
that this one run won't make enough money to pay even
half our bills."

Michele shrugged her shoulders. "So we have to do
this again. I do wish the lifepod area was large enough to
take the kids with us, but at least this is honest work."

"You know how much outfitting this cost for just one
trip," said Mark. "Yes, we have to do this again. And
again and again. This isn't any way for you to live. And
we're not preaching the gospel to anyone out here."

"Honey." Michele began massaging Mark's neck.
"We've gone over this before. We don't have any choice.
Maybe we can enlarge the living area and bring the kids

along. At least we'll get to visit with them a few weeks before we take off again. I know we didn't talk about coming out here again, but we both knew we would have to. I think everything should be paid off with two or three more trips."

"We have no idea what kind of radiation we're exposing ourselves to, what kind medical emergencies we might face or what would happen if we had a major breakdown out here. What if you get pregnant?"

Michele wrapped her arms around her husband. "The LORD will protect us."

"How is this carrying out the Great Commission?"

"I don't know, but He promised never to leave us."

A soft buzzer sounded and a yellow warning light flashed. They left their bedroom and walked down to the control room.

"Waste gas container will be full in two minutes," said the computer.

"I didn't break the suction!" cried Michele as she raced over to the control panel. She pushed the button to lift the suction tube. As the tube rose and methane stopped flowing upward, the tube became transparent.

"Jettisoning waste gases," said Mark. "Full thrusters. Computer, how full are we?"

"18%," said the computer.

There was a slight vibration.

"Storm?" asked Michele.

Mark adjusted two exterior monitors that showed a violent methane storm as the *Sojourner* expelled a stream of waste gases. The waste gases froze as they left the *Sojourner* and reliquified on hitting the upper atmosphere.

"Computer," asked Mark. "How long until all waste gases are jettisoned?"

"Two hours, eleven minutes."

"And how much longer before the storm subsides?"

"That question is outside of my design parameters."

"At least we're out of range of those gas jets from the

storm," said Mark. "I'm cutting back on the thrusters."

"How high are we?" asked Michele.

"We're thirty-two kilometers higher. The computer said that storms only reach out about 20 kilometers."

"Now it's my turn," said Michele. "I'm getting some sleep."

"I'm taking us up another twenty kilometers or so. I'll check on the garden after that," said Mark.

"The pole beans on the forty-second row and the peas on the hundred and tenth row should be ready for dinner. Leave the bees alone. The honey won't be ready until sometime on the return trip. Oh, the soy processor is low on spices. That last batch of bacon bits didn't taste quite right."

"And we need to make at least a video inspection of everything before we go down again. We've got to bring some help along next trip." Mark sat down as he spoke and stared at the monitor. All indicators turned green as the *Sojourner* settled into her new orbit.

"And one more thing," said Michele. Her blouse landed in Mark's lap. "Please don't forget to wash my clothes." He turned and her skirt hit him in the face. He chased her to the bedroom, leaving all of their clothing in the control room.

*****

Mark and Michele sat together in the control room staring at the same monitor.

"OK," asked Michele. "So what does that mean?"

"That we've almost run out of room for the short term storage of the waste gases," explained Mark. "On this trip down we will only be able to stay down twenty minutes. The next trip will be ten, then nine, then eight, then seven, then six, then several trips of around five minutes duration."

The suction tube came into contact with the upper atmosphere. Once more gaseous methane flowed up the transparent tube to the *Sojourner*.

"So how close to capacity can we come?" asked Michele.

"We're at 89% now. We can get another 4 to 6%. After that we will only be able to stay down for a few seconds at a time. We'll have to wait at least three hours before we can descend after that. With the increased mass, it's getting more difficult to control. We can't cut things as close."

"Could we jettison the waste away from us and maybe buy a few more minutes?"

"Maybe," answered Mark. "But we've increased our mass so much that we won't respond very quickly. It's too dangerous."

"So we go home with only 95% capacity."

"Agreed. That's going to really cut into our money."

"Our profits," said Michele.

"It will be several trips before we will have anything that we can remotely call 'profits'," said Mark.

*****

Michele and Mark dozed in their seats at the main control panel. A buzzer sounded and yellow warning light went off, rousing them.

"I have never seen the righteous forsaken or His seed begging bread," said Mark. "Pull it up."

He pushed a series of buttons and the suction tube pulled away from the atmosphere. Yellow lights flashed and a warning buzzer sounded as the tube became transparent.

"That's it," said Michele. "We're going home. Pull it in; lock it in place. Computer, how much methane do we have?"

"93.8% of capacity," it responded.

"Could we refine what we have and get more capacity that way?" asked Michele.

Mark shook his head. "We could, but it would take weeks. Our garden won't last that long. Besides, we have some notes due."

"Computer," asked Michele. "Please plot a course to Mars."

"That will require verification with Mars," said the computer. "We are unable to contact them without leaving our parking orbit around Titan and moving to the other side of Saturn."

Mark smiled at Michele. "We're on our way home." He touched a few buttons. The lifepod area vibrated slightly from grinding metal and the distant thrusters.

"What's frozen this time?" asked Michele.

Mark switched the monitors over to search mode. "Let's find out."

*****

"Course verification received," said the computer.

The lights came up in the bedroom, but neither Michele nor Mark moved.

"How long have we been asleep?" asked Michele.

Mark rolled over and looked at the chronometer. "Less than 5 hours."

"Ooooooooooooh!" Michele rolled over and covered her head.

"Computer," said Mark. "Store new course and implement." He punched a series of buttons on the wall and the room shifted with the sound of grinding metal. As the room tilted, they rolled out of bed.

"New course changed and implemented," said the computer. Red lights and warning buzzers replaced the white lights and silence.

"Now what?" asked Michele.

Mark hit several computer keys and came up empty. "Computer," asked Mark. "Why the warning buzzers?"

"Frozen oxygen at main thruster," said the computer.

"You're not going out there to thaw that one," said

"Don't need to," said Mark. "Just rotate the entire balloon 180%." He programmed the operation and the *Sojourner* began slowly turning with a low grinding sound.

"Why didn't the computer do that automatically?" demanded Michele. "And why did it know what the problem was this time?"

"Outside of design parameters," mimicked Mark. "Computers are stupid! Oh, there are sensors at the thrusters."

The grinding sound grew louder and the room tilted back and forth several times before stabilizing. The grinding softened, ceased.

"Can we go back to sleep now?" asked Michele.

"In a few minutes," said Mark. He approached the bed.

"No!" Michele lay back down and pulled the covers over her head.

Four

"These peas have some sort of blight on them," said Michele as she walked into the control room. "They're not going to mature."

"Last week it was the grapefruit and the week before the carrots."

"It's getting worse," said Michele. "We're going to be living completely on synthfood the last week."

"At least we have the synthfood."

"I don't trust it," said Michele. "Keep inspecting the garden carefully. *'Though the fig tree does not bud and there are no grapes on the vines, though the olive crop fails and the fields produce no food, though there are no sheep in the pen and no cattle in the stalls, yet I will rejoice in the LORD, I will be joyful in God my Savior'*...You said there was a message?"

"I've got some more bad news. Have a seat."

Michele sat down on her seat at the control panel.

"Your Mom just went home to be with the Lord. The funeral will be next week. She didn't know that she was ill until last month and she didn't want to worry us."

Michele didn't move. "Will we be close enough for a video link?"

Mark nodded and said, "There is still about a four and a half minute delay, but you should be able to watch the service without any interruptions. They won't be able to see us, however."

"It's probably best this way." She grabbed her husband and began to cry.

*****

Mark walked into the bedroom and looked at Michele. "Are you all right?"

She sat up in bed and said, "It was a beautiful service. Dad read some of her first letters to him. I didn't know that he still had them. I wish I'd been half as intelligent and mature as she was as a teenager. Several friends spoke. And Ron -- my brother Ron -- the man who never wanted anything to do with Mom's religion. He testified of her love for the Lord without being pretentious. It's been so long since I've seen Ron sober. I'll miss her, but she's much better off with the Lord. She's been in a lot of pain, but she never let anyone know it. If only I can have the testimony she has."

"That's wonderful," said Mark. "Would you like some good news?"

"The shock of something new and different might kill me. You know that new things always take some getting used to. Don't you care about the health of your poor wife? I might just keel over from shock. Why ..."

"...Don't you come over here and look at this and stop talking?"

Michele got out of bed and walked across the room to the monitor. She didn't read it correctly the first time, so she adjusted the screen and blinked at it for a few seconds.

Michele squealed and hugged Mark. "You sold it! The entire load to one buyer?"

"And this is to a wholesaler," said Mark. "It's a locked floor price. It could be more when we dock."

"Why? How come? I mean . . . what would justify this?"

"That bothers me too," said Mark. "We've neglected the news. We haven't even bothered to store the free stuff."

"How much will we have to pay for oxygen for the next trip? How about a new garden? And another suction tube?"

"Victor didn't have prices for all that, but he said that

he could get them for us for less than we paid going out."

Michele put both of her hands on Mark's shoulders and said, "Victor? Victor Lattimore?"

Mark nodded and they both fell silent for several seconds.

Michele found her voice first. "Victor Latimore is our jobber? Why do the royals want to buy our methane? And why are they willing to sell to us?"

"Maybe it's nothing more than the fact that we succeeded where they failed and they want on the bandwagon."

Michele cocked her head slightly and looked straight into Mark's eyes, but she was lost deep in thought. "The royals would do that, but not Victor. We're 'way too small for him. Did you make the deal with Victor personally or just with his office?"

"With Victor personally. He called us, and when he called he knew about your Mom."

"That's not the same Victor I dated twenty-five years ago."

"The Lord can work in anyone's heart. Maybe he's changed. Do you mistrust him?"

"He's trustworthy. It's just that he's married to the empire. Now that's not such a bad thing, but he's not the least bit interested in anything that isn't furthering the Constitutional Empire. When we were trying to go outbound, that didn't include us. We need to find out what changed. Did you even check on the current market price of methane?"

"Victor was the first one to call and his price was so good that when he offered to do all the service work, I didn't even care what other jobbers would give us."

"What do you mean, 'do all the service work'?'"

"This price includes docking at the Royal base on Deimos. While we take a two-week break, they will begin re-outfitting the *Sojourner*. Before we leave again we must spend two weeks training some Royals for a few balloons they've built."

Michele shook her head and dropped her arms. "The Royals have built their own balloons? That's a switch. I can still remember Sir Cramer saying, 'We don't see any immediate need for new fuel sources. We can't stop you from going on your own, but remember, you're on your own.' Did Victor even give you any hints as to the change of heart?"

"Nothing," said Mark. "The only thing that I noticed was that he wasn't his old chipper self. Something was eating at him."

"Did you make a firm deal or just an intent?"

"Oh, I was willing to shop around until he threw in the service. I've always wondered what it would be like getting the best."

"Just the same, I'm calling up a history of methane prices since we've been gone."

"Just what you need. Something else to do."

"Relax. I'll be done in an hour."

"At least there's nothing left of the garden to tend."

Five

Mark entered the doorway to the control room from the outside. As he took off the tanks and suit, he gave Michele a report.

"Everything checks out OK. The Lord has blessed us with no measurable methane losses. Stopping the heat losses must have taken care of that. There were several frozen lines, but they're flowing now. Did your search turn up anything?"

"That's weird..." murmured Michele.

'Weird: of or pertaining to the supernatural.' You find something spooky in all those numbers?"

"Maybe I have."

"This I gotta see."

"That's just it. There's nothing to see. Prices rose steadily, but only slightly until a couple of weeks ago. The Royals are paying nearly double market price. I just don't get it. For what?"

"Well stop and think. What are they getting out of this? Our good will?"

"Hardly," sniffed Michele. "The Lunar delegation would probably like to confiscate everything we own under the guise of some new taxes. That's exactly what they did to the Cortez. If it had come back, it would have been seized for taxes without the royals ever putting a dime into it. Why should they care what we think?"

"I don't know, but it's rather obvious that they do."

"So what are they getting out of this?" asked Michele.

"As much methane as possible as soon as possible," replied Mark.

"So why is that important?" persisted Michele.

"Basic economics: quantity and or quality of product."

"What's fueling the demand?"

"Oh no you don't," objected Mark. "We haven't got enough time to search for some two-paragraph story buried on page two hundred ten of three weeks ago's info sheet."

"Did you ask Victor?"

Mark stopped momentarily and said, "No."

"He'll tell me," said Michele confidently.

"If he knows."

"Victor will know. Call him up."

"When?"

"Right now."

"OK," said Mark. He sat down and began typing. Victor's face appeared on the monitor in seconds.

"Victor?" Mark raised his eyebrows. "Thanks for the quick response."

"Why are you giving us this deal?" asked Michele. To her Victor seemed much the same as when she had last seen him about ten years ago. His black hair bore some traces of gray and the lines above his brown eyes had gotten quite heavy. She saw, as Mark had, that he was bothered by something. His laugh in response to her question was nervous.

"You're as direct as ever," said Victor. "I thought a few decades of marriage would mellow you somewhat."

"So what's the deal?" demanded Michele.

"I'm not allowed to tell you," responded Victor. "What I can tell you is that you'd better not shop around."

"Why?" queried Michele.

"Some people want to seize your ship outright," said Victor. "I was able to convince them that you would be far more disposed to help us -- and we must have your help -- if you were persuaded and not coerced."

"So you're not going to let us shop around?" asked Mark.

"We cannot stop you from doing anything you want, but they will make you sorry if you resist."

"Resist?" echoed Mark.

"Poor choice of words, please forgive me." Victor smiled and the screen went blank.

"Have they got any information about Titan's atmosphere that we don't have?" wondered Mark.

"What? Why? What difference does that make?" sputtered Michele.

"They either want the methane or they want something that we're bringing back as an impurity. Since we don't know ourselves what's mixed in, do they know something we don't?"

"No!" insisted Michele. "I mean, of course we can't know everything someone else knows, but we've studied this for years. Every probe sent out contradicted every other probe. They can't be sure of anything."

"So they need the methane."

"And we need the money. Sounds like a good market economy. We also need to stay alive."

"The Royals don't murder to get their way," said Mark.

"They tax," said Michele. "And taxes can murder by slow starvation."

"So you think that we should take their offer and not try to find out why?"

"I don't think that we have much choice," said Michele. "We certainly don't have enough time to look for hidden clues."

A yellow warning light flashed on the central control panel.

"You're certainly right about that," said Mark. He left the room. He came back to pick up some tools and left again.

Six

The computer spoke in complete darkness. "Docking to Deimos in four hours, twenty-seven minutes. Weightlessness commences in four hours, 8 minutes. Speed matched to Deimos, clearance granted, docking collar extended and ready. Request from Deimos for docking collar matching information. This information is classified and must be transmitted manually. Please advise."

Mark sat up in bed and Michele rolled over. The lights began to glow.

"Please advise!" roared Mark. "I have no idea what our docking collar info is. Where would I find it?"

"Muffh," said Michele.

"Come on!" Mark shook his wife. "Do you know where the docking collar information is?"

"Sorry, no idea," said Michele without moving.

Mark jumped out of bed, went across the bedroom to the control panel and sat down. He stared at the panel, opened a drawer, pulled out a disk and inserted it.

"Found it," He called out. He typed a few seconds and the lifepod area vibrated to the sound of grinding metal. The room shifted and the lights came up to full. The control panel beeped.

"Now what?" said Mark sharply.

An unfamiliar face, a very young man with close-cropped blond hair and blue eyes came up on the monitor.

"That's not a very Christlike attitude," chided Michele as she entered the room.

"You're right," said Mark. "Please forgive me."

He touched the panel and the image on the monitor began speaking.

"This is Lieutenant Junior Grade Phillip Edwards. Your docking collar information is either incomplete or inaccurate. I have been ordered to make a physical inspection, so please make ready for boarding in fifteen minutes." The screen went blank.

"Up and dressed," said Mark. "We're having company."

"Noooooooooooooo. You guys have your meeting. Let me sleep."

Mark pulled clothes out of a drawer and threw them at her.

"Put some clothes on."

*****

As they dressed, they watched a shuttlecraft approach the *Sojourner*. As it fastened to the *Sojourner*'s side, a suited figure got out and entered through the exterior air lock.

Mark and Michele entered the control room as the man they had seen onscreen, dressed in an officer's uniform, stepped through the doorway from outside.

"Phil Edwards," he introduced himself with a smile. "May I see the disk with your docking collar information on it, please?"

Mark handed it to him.

"We have very little time," said Phil. "I can examine this as we go."

"Go where?" asked Michele.

"To physically examine your docking collar," said Phil.

"But that's in the core!" protested Michele.

"Which is why we need to hurry," said Phil. Mark pulled out a suit and began to get into it. Michele balked.

"There's no need for both of us to go..." she argued.

"If everything checks out," said Phil.

"I'll just stay here and watch on monitor," Michele

persisted.

"But if everything does not check out, you should both be present to sign any necessary change orders. Please, we have very little time."

"Humor him, please," said Mark.

"Oh, all right," grumbled Michele. She suited up and they left for the core.

They walked in silence. As they approached the core, the roar of the intermittent burners would have made conversation impossible. They continued walking until the nearest burner cut out.

"Here's your original disk and a correct copy," said Phil. "All I did was make a copy of your disk and corrupt yours."

"So what's going...?" started Michele. Phil put his finger to his lips.

"There's very little time, so please just listen. Victor has been jailed for negotiating and signing that contract of yours. But there's nothing the Council can do to change the terms, since it's countersigned by the king himself. What really infuriated the Council is the automatic renewal clause. That was his majesty's own idea."

"What is going on?" asked Michele again.

Phil continued, laughing. "I was picked for this assignment because I've been so apolitical. I really don't know what the argument at the bottom of it is all about. But I did some snooping around. You'll need the disk to cover me. When my superiors ask about my visit, don't waste time lying to them. They'd know anyway. Just show them the two disks and let them draw their own conclusions. Oh, by the way, I examined your docking coupling before seeing you and it'll work without any problem."

The near burner came on, so they walked away from it until they could hear again.

Phil continued. "Any news item you choose to print will be monitored. You're safe so long as Lunar

Councilmen Kennedy and Rockefeller believe that you don't know anything."

"They're correct," said Mark. "We have no idea what's going on. But the Lord has protected us so far and He will continue to protect us."

"You sound like you really believe that," said Phil. "Well, you certainly need protection from someone in high places. Let me explain what I think's going on.

"Every colony has a limited number of natural resources. Now, the colonies can trade with each other, but most of the trading is done with Earth. And that means almost everything that we mine, make or buy comes through the original Lunar Colony. Sure, there's been some expansion, but it was so expensive that the government had to finance it. So the government owns everything. Oh, there are some real small private businesses, but the government owns everything that's important. And no one has a choice.

"The Council talks about how free we are because we can vote for anyone we want. But the only people who have any money are the ones who do everything the government tells them. And even some of them wind up like your friend Victor."

"A friend that I haven't seen for over a decade," said Michele.

"Believe me," said Phil. "He really is your best friend."

"So what can we do to help him?" asked Mark.

Phil pulled a tape recorder out of his pocket.

"Listen to this tape," said Phil. "The first voice you'll hear is Councilman Kennedy. The next man is Councilman Rockefeller. This was taped by the king in a closed meeting of the entire Council." Phil pressed a button on the player. Michele and Mark listened to the voice of Councilman Kennedy.

"These greedy balloonists are an ultra-rich aristocracy. They lack any compassion for their less fortunate fellow colonists and are attempting to exploit them by shackling them into economic slavery. This is just how the oil companies of ancient Earth treated their fellow countrymen. We must not allow these misers to repeat this shameful Dark Age. If we act now, before it is too late, we can protect the many who depend on us from the dreadful pit of economic slavery."

"Every moment we delay," continued the voice of Councilman Rockefeller, "the insidious poison of greed gnaws more deeply at our fellow colonists. We fled the ravages of greed-hardened Earth and her wars -- wars which fueled the unholy passions and lusts for other people's property. If we allow these same lusts and passions to be rekindled in the Imperial realms, we can expect nothing better than a repeat of the wars of history's cruelest tyrants. We will languish in the cold, passionless grip of greed. If these balloonists had paid their fair share of taxes, they would be unable to exploit their fellow colonists in this way."

"It is not too late," spoke Kennedy's voice again. "Even at this dark hour. Every minute we delay, every day we falter brings us that much closer to the bloodshed of senseless greed from which our founders in their wisdom hoped to shield us."

Phil shut off the tape and said, "Now this is just my idea. But I think that they're afraid of the hope that you've given people. You don't owe anything to the government. Take their money, because you have to, but don't sell out to them.

"You want to help Victor? Leave as soon as possible and keep going back as long as you have strength. Finance as many independents as you can."

Phil hurled both the tape and recorder into a roaring burner.

"And take your children with you. You don't want to leave any potential hostages."

Phil hugged them. "As long as you keep going, we're winning. Please, don't quit."

The best gift you can give an author is an honest, thoughtful review. Please consider leaving one online. Help us understand what you liked and didn't like about the book and why. Help authors reach more readers and spread your influence and ours. If you liked the book, please recommend it to your spouse, friends, pastors, teachers, cashiers, employers, – anybody and everybody you see each day. If you don't know what to say, remember Proverb 16:3 – Commit thy works unto the Lord and thy thoughts shall be established. Thank you!

OTHER BOOKS AND PRODUCTS FROM FINDLEY FAMILY VIDEO PUBLICATIONS

All our books (including Historical Fiction, SciFi, contemporary relationships short stories, and an Archaeological Mystery serial) are linked on our website, Findley Family Video Publications, https://findleyfamilyvideopublications.com/

Our blog, *Elk Jerky for the Soul,* includes posts on current issues, excerpts from our fiction and nonfiction works, Bible teaching, travel and everyday observations, and more.

Visit our YouTube Channel https://www.youtube.com/channel/UCGhwNpU115ARM wgYwTIJBrA/featured. Book trailers, video excerpts, project teasers, and more.

Science, history, literature, and biblical authority studies are the focus of our book and video projects.

Historical Fiction

by Michael J. Findley
The Ephron the Hittite Series (Including boxed set of all titles)
Ephron Son of Zohar
Tawananna Daughter of Zohar
Heth Son of Canaan Son of Ham, Noah
Shelometh Daughter of Yovov Wife of Ephron
Zita Son of Ephron and Shelometh

Adult Romantic Suspense
by Mary C. Findley

The Men of the Realmlands series

Book One: The Baron's Ring
The Captain's Blade

Send a White Rose

Chasing the Texas Wind

Carrie's Hired Hand (novella)

Young Adult Historical Adventure
by Mary C. Findley

Hope and the Knight of the Black Lion (plus illustrated version)

The Benny and the Bank Robber Series

Benny and the Bank Robber (Plus homeschool editions for student and teacher with review and vocabulary)
Doctor Dad
The Oregon Sentinel
Lines in Pleasant Places

Science Fiction

by Michael J. Findley
The Empire Saga (five of six of the following books in one volume)

City on a Hill (Novelette)
Sojourner (Short Story)

[*Nehemiah LLC* (Full-length novel excluded from the boxed set due to length and only available as a standalone ebook, paperback, and hardcover versions)]

Empire One: Humiliation
Empire Two: Repentance
Empire Three: Sanctification

Steampunk

by Sophronia Belle Lyon (pen name for Mary C. Findley)
The Alexander Legacy Steampunk Literary Tribute Series
Book One: A Dodge, a Twist, and a Tobacconist

(including illustrated version)
Book Two: The Pinocchio Factor
Book Three: The Most Dangerous Game
Book Four: Beware the Bustle

Fantasy/Allegory

by Mary C. Findley

Allegorical clockwork novella inspired by Little Red Riding Hood
The Acolyte's Education

A Paranormal Urban Fantasy serial
His Sign: The Wait Is Over
His Sign 2: The Ezra Solution

Contemporary Fiction

by Mary C. Findley

Romantic Suspense Novella
Fall On Your Knees

Relationships Short Stories
Fifty Shades of Faithful
Fifty Shades of Faithful 2: In Living Color

The Great Thirst Serial Archaeological Mystery
(including boxed set of all titles)
Part One: Prepared
Part Two: Purified
Part Three: Pursued
Part Four: Persecuted
Part Five: Persevering
Part Six: Protected
The Great Thirst Part Seven: Prevailing

Murder Mystery
Mapped Out Murders

Nonfiction

by Mary C. Findley

Write for the King of Glory, 2nd Edition (updated, with tips on indie writing and publishing)

by Michael J. and Mary C. Findley

The Good, the Bad, and the Ugly: A Readers' and Writers' Guide for Believers

Biblical Studies (Teacher and student editions plus excerpts in OT and NT Manuscript History)

Antidisestablishmentarianism (illustrated and plain versions)

Serial versions, illustrated and plain
What Is an Establishment of Religion?
What Is Secular Humanism?
What Is Science?
What Are the Results of the Establishment of Secular Humanism?

The Conflict of the Ages series (All have teacher and student editions plus one combined teacher edition for 1-3)

I. The Scientific History of Origins
II. The Origin of Evil in the World that Was
III. They Deliberately Forgot: The Flood and the Ice Age
IV. Ice Age Civilizations
V. The Ancient World

by Michael J. Findley
Short Recaps of longer nonfiction works
(*Antidisestablishmentarianism* and *Conflict of the Ages*
Disestablish: An Overview from Creation to the Ice Age
Under the Sun: The Truth about History from the Beginning

*****

Christian Books in Multiple Genres. Join Christian Indie Author ~ Readers Group on Facebook.
https://www.facebook.com/groups/291215317668431/